JOHN BLACKBURN

Colonel Bogus

I0633518

VALANCOURT BOOKS

Colonel Bogus by John Blackburn
Originally published in Great Britain by Jonathan Cape in 1964
First U.S. edition published by Mill and Morrow in 1964 under the title
Packed for Murder
First Valancourt Books edition 2025

Published by Valancourt Books, Richmond, Virginia
http://www.valancourtbooks.com

ISBN 978-1-960241-57-3 (*trade paperback*)
Also available as an electronic book.

Cover by Pedro Marques
Set in Dante MT

COLONEL BOGUS

JOHN BLACKBURN was born in 1923 in the village of Corbridge, England, the second son of a clergyman. Blackburn attended Haileybury College near London beginning in 1937, but his education was interrupted by the onset of World War II; the shadow of the war, and that of Nazi Germany, would later play a role in many of his works. He served as a radio officer during the war in the Mercantile Marine from 1942 to 1945, and resumed his education afterwards at Durham University, earning his bachelor's degree in 1949. Blackburn taught for several years after that, first in London and then in Berlin, and married Joan Mary Clift in 1950. Returning to London in 1952, he took over the management of Red Lion Books.

It was there that Blackburn began writing, and the immediate success in 1958 of his first novel, *A Scent of New-Mown Hay*, led him to take up a career as a writer full time. He and his wife also maintained an antiquarian bookstore, a secondary career that would inform some of Blackburn's work, including the bibliomystery *Blue Octavo* (1963). *A Scent of New-Mown Hay* typified the approach that would come to characterize Blackburn's twenty-eight novels, which defied easy categorization in their unique and compelling mixture of the genres of science fiction, horror, mystery, and thriller. Many of Blackburn's best novels came in the late 1960s and early 1970s, with a string of successes that included the classics *A Ring of Roses* (1965), *Children of the Night* (1966), *Nothing but the Night* (1968; adapted for a 1973 film starring Christopher Lee and Peter Cushing), *Devil Daddy* (1972) and *Our Lady of Pain* (1974). Somewhat unusually for a popular horror writer, Blackburn's novels were not only successful with the reading public but also won widespread critical acclaim: the *Times Literary Supplement* declared him 'today's master of horror' and compared him with the Grimm Brothers, while the *Penguin Encyclopedia of Horror and the Supernatural* regarded him as 'certainly the best British novelist in his field' and the *St James Guide to Crime & Mystery Writers* called him 'one of England's best practicing novelists in the tradition of the thriller novel'.

By the time Blackburn published his final novel in 1985, much of his work was already out of print, an inexplicable neglect that continued until Valancourt began republishing his novels in 2013. John Blackburn died in 1993.

PROLOGUE

"I'll tell you nothing, gentlemen—nothing at all." Though the woman was old and haggard and seemed ill, there was a great strength and dignity in her ravaged face. "If you think there is anything else to destroy, you can look for it yourselves."

"But that's most unfriendly of you, madam." Captain "Topper" Tree, late of the Queen's Own Northumbrian Borderers, smiled, but he wasn't really enjoying himself, for he liked them to be easy. He liked to see them break down and plead. To crawl and scrabble on the floor in front of him, weeping. This old bitch wouldn't crawl in a hundred years, he decided. Not if he beat her—not if he threatened to burn her alive.

"Yes, really most unfriendly." His walking stick tapped against the toe of his shoe, and the little dark moustache grown in honour of Lord Alexander curled slightly to show a line of badly stained teeth.

"But come on, Princess. Be a sport and save the boys work. Is there any more of this incriminating rubbish hidden in the house?" He glanced at the little pile of papers on the table beside him; torn envelopes and faded manuscripts and letters that had been written a long time ago.

"Look for yourselves, gentlemen. But answer me one question first." The thin lips almost spat out the word *gentlemen*. "How did my country sink low enough to employ excrement like you?"

"Excrement! That's not very polite of you, madam." Tree's eyes still smiled, but there was a row of slogans behind them now. "Niggers begin at Calais. . . . The Foreigner is no good." Too right they weren't any good. They were all the same, rotten to the core, and God, how he hated them.

"No, that was very, very rude indeed." His stick tapped

5

twice more and then stopped tapping. He raised it, grinned at it, and then his muscles hardened and it came forward in a swinging, backhanded arc towards the woman's throat. Her old worn body made hardly a sound as it crumpled to the floor.

"Excrement! She called us filth. Shouldn't have done that, should she?" He bent over the bundle of rags and then looked up at the man beside him.

"Yes, I'm afraid I've killed her, old boy. Sorry about it. Didn't mean to, but I came all over queer, as they say. Still, it doesn't really matter, and the chances are that we've got all her damned letters. That's what we'll tell our employers anyway." Tree leaned on his stick for a moment, breathing deeply. As always happened when he was angry the old wound in his back seemed to burn as though the shrapnel that had made it were still there.

"And now let's get on with Phase Two of the operation and dispose of her body." He watched his companion lift the thin shoulders, and then his own body stiffened. Somewhere below them a bell had begun to ring.

CHAPTER ONE

"Sure you've got the right road, Wilson?" Mr. Robert Herod, senior partner of Hyde, Herod & Scott, auctioneers, valuers, and estate agents, scowled over his steering wheel at the dingy cul-de-sac which was opening up before him and the other two men. "Looks a pretty unlikely neighbourhood to me."

"Yes, I'm afraid this is it, sir. Benham Grove—Number 32." The clerk at his side consulted a street map. "Should be the last house on the right."

"Well, let's have a look, shall we?" Herod brought the car to a halt and climbed heavily out. He made a fine imposing figure in his dark broadcloth suit, the bowler hat set at exact right-angles to his polished jowls, and the chain of a presentation watch sparkling merrily in the sunlight.

"No," Herod said, removing a pipe from his mouth and knocking it out against the gate post. "No, not at all what I should care to describe as a 'Desirable Residence.'"

"No indeed, sir." Wilson hurried across the pavement and followed Herod's gaze. The garden was a ruin of weeds and overgrown bushes, and the house didn't look as though it had seen a workman near it for years. "No, not at all the class of property we're accustomed to deal with, Mr. Herod."

"You can say that again, Wilson." Herod shook his head in ponderous disapproval of the disrepair in front of them. A run of slates was missing from the roof, a line of loose guttering sagged beneath the eaves, and at least three window panes were broken.

"Still it's a public trustee job and, as you know, it doesn't do to refuse them. 'Needs must when the devil drives,' eh? It seems that the old lady left no will, and they haven't been able to trace a single relative. All very, very sad. . . . Get a move on there, Fred, we haven't got all day"—this to a labourer who was removing his tools from the trunk of the car.

"Just coming, guv." With infinite slowness the man dragged his case across the pavement and looked at the house. "Blimey," he said, "the old bitch couldn't 'arf do with a lick of paint."

"She could indeed, Fred, but that's no concern of ours." Herod peered into the bowl of his pipe, blew down the stem, sniffed at it, and pushed it lovingly away into the depths of his pocket. "As I told you, we've only been asked to dispose of the contents. Wright, Brown & Turpin are stuck with the property itself, I'm glad to say, and the best of British luck to them.

"Now, where's this wretched fellow from the police station who was to come round with the keys? Dawdling about drinking tea as usual, I suppose. No respect for the ratepayers' money. Let's go and see if we can get in by ourselves." He pulled back the sagging gate and marched pompously down the path with his retinue at his heels.

"Good morning, Alderman." The policeman hurried

round from the back of the house, where he had been enjoying a quiet smoke. He was young and ambitious, and at the moment his face was set in a wide beam of welcome, for he knew that Herod was a power in the land: Chairman of the Housing Committee and earmarked as the next mayor, secretary of the Rotarians, past Master of the Masonic Lodge. The kind of man it was important to keep in with if one desired promotion.

"Should I open up for you, sir?"

"Yes, of course, open up, Constable." Herod frowned both at the man's slowness and at the scribbled messages on the porch. "Wendy loves Sam. . . . Jimmy Dainter is a coward. . . . Children and—" he moved his foot hurriedly to one side "—and dogs."

"There we are, sir." The policeman turned the lock and threw back the door to reveal nothing but darkness and a thick, stale smell made up of damp, woodrot, and the dust of months.

"Yes, there we are indeed." Herod paused in the doorway, thinking of his suit. "Just get yourself in there, Fred, and throw open a few shutters. No point in groping about in the dark."

"As you say, guv." The man walked mournfully past him; a few seconds later there came a crash of rusty bolts, and a thin stream of grey sunlight peered through the windows.

"Ah, that's better, though I can't say I'm impressed by what I see." Herod stared into the hall and then stepped forward. The boards felt soft and spongy under his feet as though they might give way at any moment, and he could imagine the grey jackets of dry rot which would be clustered around the joists that held them.

"No, not at all impressive." The carpet was almost mouldering on the floor, the Victorian furniture was covered by a layer of dust, and from everywhere came the stale smell of neglect. "How long did you say it was since this place was lived in, Constable?"

"Almost six months to the day it must be, Alderman, since the old lady disappeared."

"Well, there's more than six months' accumulation of filth here. Did she live quite alone?" Herod drew on a pair of leather gloves and rubbed his hand across the top of a table. Quite a nice piece of walnut, he thought, but who buys that kind of sham Jacobean horror these days?

"Yes, quite alone, sir. That's what made it so difficult, you see. No friends or relatives we could question. Nobody to tell us anything about her, except that Russian *emigré* organization she belonged to, and they were the reverse of helpful. All we found out for sure was that she got on a train to Edinburgh on the night of January the thirtieth, and never arrived at the other end. You must have read about the case, sir."

"I read about it all right—what you blighters allowed 'em to print, that is." Herod considered what he knew about the late owner of the house. A very tall, gaunt, and rather frightening old woman who had come to the town ten years ago but seemed to have made no friends, though she was often seen in the streets, hurrying to the station or browsing before the windows of antique shops. A figure of curiosity when she had first arrived, but soon something that was odd but accepted, like the vicar's dancing limp or old Colonel Martin's tendency to march about talking loudly to himself.

"Quite, sir, and between you and I, they weren't allowed to print much." The constable leaned forward confidentially. The thud of heavy boots told him that the labourer was at work upstairs, and the clerk had slung a writing board over his shoulders and seemed oblivious to everything except the inventory.

"Very 'ush 'ush about it the inspector was, Alderman, but I did gather there was more in the case than meets the eye. Seems that the Special Branch was brought in, or so one of the C.I.D. boys told me."

"Special Branch!" Herod's thoughts were half on what the man was telling him and half on the little Dupleis clock on the mantlepiece. He seemed to remember selling it to her himself a couple of years or so ago. She'd been quite a frequent visitor at his salerooms, bidding for the end lots which nobody else wanted—books mainly, bric-a-brac, junk of all kinds. Yes, he distinctly remembered selling her this clock. Three pounds ten, she'd paid for it, though it wouldn't fetch anything like that in its present state. The dial was green with damp and most probably the works would be gummed up as well.

"The Special Branch, Constable?" he said, raising his eyebrows slightly. "But that's spies and so on, isn't it? I think your friend at the C.I.D. must have been having a joke. How could old Tania Vitgeft possibly have been mixed up in anything like that?"

"I dunno, sir. All I can say is that there was something funny about the business. I mean how they presumed she was dead so quickly, and putting 'er stuff up for auction after only six months."

"Well, I'm sure your superiors know what they're doing, Constable, and the fact remains that she had debts—a great many debts." Herod raised a great flabby hand to drive home the point. "She owed money to the gas and electricity companies, to local tradesmen who cannot afford to wait, to the council for rates. Debts which must be paid, Constable, and which my firm is instructed to see are paid.

"But tell me something if you can. This title of hers—'Princess.' Do you happen to know if it was genuine?" The picture of a tastefully got-up catalogue flitted through Herod's mind as he spoke—"Messrs. Hyde, Herod & Scott have pleasure in offering for sale by public auction the contents of Number 32, Benham Grove, the property of the late Princess Tania Vitgeft." By the look of the hall the house would contain little of value, but a title might liven up the bidding considerably.

"Well, I couldn't rightly say, sir, though I never heard it wasn't genuine. All the same, some of these foreign ladies, Poles, Russians, and so on, do seem to have a mighty lot of titles among 'em."

"Yes, I'm afraid those are my views as well." The image of

the catalogue faded from Herod's mind. Most probably Tania
Vitgeft had merely been a princess in her own mind, and he
couldn't risk using that kind of publicity.

"Well, what have you got there, Wilson? Anything of interest?" He turned to his clerk, who was bending over a little writing desk.

"No, not really, sir. A nice bit of fake Sheraton, but a pretty
good fake. Bad attack of woodworm, though."

"Yes, so there is." Herod's gloved finger prodded the side
of the desk and was rewarded with a cascade of white dust.
"Active, too, I'm sorry to say. 'The worm that dieth not,' as the
good book has it. An attractive phrase, though untrue in this
case. A dollop of D.D.T. will do for these little blighters. Finished in here now?"

"Yes, sir, it's all down." Wilson made a final note and turned
over a sheet.

"Good. Then let's go next door and see what treasures we
shall find." Herod turned and smiled at the policeman. "Well,
it's been most kind of you to let us in, Officer, but there's no
need to hang about any longer. When you get back to the station please give my respects to Inspector Probert. Tell him I
hope to see him at the Rotary dinner next Wednesday."

"I'll do that, sir." The constable handed him the keys. "The
inspector told me to say that if there's anything else you need,
will you please let us know."

"Thank you again, Officer, and we'll get in touch with you
if there is." Herod watched him move out through the door;
then he followed Wilson into the next room. From above his
head came a series of crashes followed by a curse. One of the
upstairs doors must have sagged on its hinges and Fred was
having to prize it open.

"Now, contents of the library," he said, glancing round him.
"And most of the books will be junk, I should imagine." He
crossed to the first of three tall cases and studied the faded
spines. No, not junk, he decided, not entirely junk, though
there wasn't anything to write home about either. Although

books rarely fetched much at the sales, he was interested in them and very knowledgeable. His eyes ran across the shelves as Wilson listed the rest of the room.

Yes, quite a pretty little set of Dickens there, though the late owner hadn't been much of a hand at polishing. Under their layer of dust the covers had a harsh, brittle look and would probably crack if they were opened too far. *The Collected Works of Sir Walter Scott, Bart.*, bound in heavy, unmanageable morocco; he'd have a job getting rid of that little number. An outdated *Britannica* in India paper. He pulled out the first volume and glanced hopefully at the title page. Good, the eleventh edition. They should get a quid or two for that.

And here in the second case quite an interesting little collection of books on the Russo-Japanese war of 1905. Yes, really quite interesting. Here was Priboi's *Battle of Tsushima*, and in better condition than one usually could find it. *The Sea of Japan*, by Nicholas Klado; pretty scarce that, he seemed to remember. Semenoff's *Rasplata*; should be worth a fiver of anyone's money. Jane's *Imperial Russian Navy*. Yes, quite a nice little hoard, though a strange subject for an old lady to have collected, even if she were Russian.

"See that the books are well mixed up when you come to list 'em," he said, grinning at Wilson who was on his knees before a sideboard. "We don't want the dealers carrying off anything that's any good and leaving us with the rubbish."

"I'll do that, sir." Wilson got up and started to beat the dust from his trousers. "Nothing in here, I'm afraid. Thought I'd got a couple of Spode plates for a second, but they're sham all right. Belgian by the look of 'em."

"Um, a pity. It's a long time since I had the pleasure of selling any Spode. One or two nice books in there at a first glance, but very little else. From what I've seen so far I rather doubt if the entire contents will fetch more than three hundred. Still, 'ours not to reason why,' as the poet has it—though if this hadn't been a public trustee job I wouldn't have touched it. Now, let's get a move on." Herod consulted the plan of the house which the police had given him. "I see that the next room is rather sinisterly marked *parlour*."

Slowly and carefully, for they were that kind of men, Herod and Wilson worked their way through the house like two stately vultures picking clean a corpse. They missed very little, but there was very little to miss; unsaleable furniture, and unmatched china, and corroded crockery which looked as though it had been picked up in back-street junk shops. Herod felt extremely put out as at last they climbed the stairs to the second floor. It really was too bad, he thought, that a man of his standing should be subjected to this.

But, if the ground floor had been uncared for, upstairs the house was a nightmare. There the dust lay, not in layers, but in thick fungoid growths, the wallpaper hung in sodden strips, and the floor of the landing felt so rotten that he feared for his safety. Old people living alone, he thought. Old, slightly crazy people with no relatives, no friends, and nobody to clear up for them. Dust and decay and utter helplessness. He crossed into the first of the bedrooms, and pulled open the big oak wardrobe with its smell of mothballs and must and the sight of long black dresses which six months ago had swept the pavements to the terror or mirth of children. He closed it quickly and then looked round as Fred appeared in the doorway.

"Could you spare us a moment, guv? There's a couple of trunks through here and one of 'em's padlocked. All right if I bust it open?" There was a look of pleasurable anticipation on the man's face; he obviously enjoyed busting things.

"Yes, of course you can break it open." Herod dismissed him with a nod and peered around the rest of the room. The bed and dressing-table were quite worthless, but the marble-topped washstand might fetch a few pounds. Very fashionable they had become of late—very "U," though he couldn't for the life of him think why. He left Wilson to make the inventory and moved next door as a crack of breaking metal sounded like a gun shot.

"Gawd, guv, she didn't 'arf go off with a bang." Fred with-

drew his screwdriver from the shattered lock and, before
Herod could restrain him, tipped the trunk on its side. A pile
of books poured out on the floor, raising a thick cloud of dust
as they did so. "Junk," Fred said contemptuously. "Just a load
of ruddy junk."

"Yes, you're probably right, but there's no need to suppose
so till we've had a look at them. What's in the second trunk?
... Books too. Well, take them out one by one and stack them
properly." Herod spoke out of the interests of discipline, but
as he looked at the sorry pile on the floor he knew that Fred
was right. These really were just rubbish. Cracked Victorian
calf, sermons and tracts, Hood's *Poetical Works* with the spines
ripped off. The collection of somebody who had hoarded like
a magpie without taste or knowledge.

"'Oly Bible, Volume One. 'Oly Bible, Volume Two. Smith's
Family Dictionary." Fred pulled out the contents of the second
trunk, muttering the titles aloud as he did so. *"The Pilgrim's
Progress*, illustrated by Doré. We 'ad one of them last week;
fetched 'arf a quid it did. An' 'ere's a ruddy great *Times Atlas*
wedged right across. Take me a minute to get the bitch
loose. . . . Ker-ist—Jesus Ker-ist." The man's voice seemed to
choke and then die out as though the dust were stifling him.

"What's that? You think you may have found something?"
Herod swung round with a gleam of excitement in his face.
It immediately turned to deep concern as he looked at his
employee. Fred was leaning over the side of the trunk, staring
down into it and breathing deeply.

"Fred," Herod said, "Fred lad, what's the matter?" The old
boy must have strained himself breaking that lock and been
taken ill. "Fred, what is it?" Herod was a smug, self-important
man, but still one of the few excuses for a capitalist system: the
employer who really cared for the welfare of his workpeople.
He hurried across and put an arm round the man's shoulder.

"But it'll be all right," he said. "Go and get some fresh air
and you'll be as right as rain." He pulled Fred back and, as he
did so, his own eyes looked down into the trunk and he knew

that it was no strain or stroke that bothered Fred, but the thing he was looking at. A thing like a horrible leather doll with its wizened face staring up through the gap in the books which had covered it and hands that had shrunk to claws still tearing at the sides of the trunk which was its coffin.

"Ah, there you are." Herod looked up and stared drunkenly at Wilson, who had appeared in the doorway. "Get out of here and find a phone box. Then ring up those idle bastards at the police station and tell them to come round quick.

"What's that? Yes, of course something's wrong—terribly wrong. Old Tania Vitgeft didn't disappear on any train to Scotland. She died here and we've just found her."

CHAPTER TWO

Although the weather was hot, even for August, the office windows were tightly closed and an enormous electric fire glowed in the grate. The heat beat on the frosted-glass partition of the secretary's cubicle, making life misery for Miss Florrie Bond as she turned over the piles of reports before her, but to General Kirk, head of Her Majesty's Foreign Office Intelligence, it was a near approach to heaven.

Well, what is it now? he wondered, lowering the cigar with which he had been thickening the already overpowering atmosphere as a telephone sounded dully through the partition and Florrie came into the room. A nice girl, he thought, a nice, jolly, decorative girl, but not quite up to the job yet. She should know by now that he never accepted calls during the first hour of the afternoon. His own secretary was away for a fortnight, called to the bedside of an aged parent, and on her advice Florrie had been promoted from the outer office as a temporary stopgap. Though Kirk liked her as a person, he found her extremely inefficient and regretted Miss Colman's recommendation almost as much as her absence. If she didn't return to work soon, he decided, he would have to look for another replacement.

"It's Mr. Trubenoff, sir. He said that he was very sorry to disturb you, but could you spare him a few minutes." The girl's voice was low and secretive; she obviously enjoyed the cloak-and-dagger atmosphere of her job.

"Igor Trubenoff." Kirk frowned slightly. "How very strange of him. He knows perfectly well that I don't like visitors at this time of the day. But tell him to come up if he must." He picked up the cigar again and a cloud of grey smoke drifted to the ceiling.

The man who came into the room a moment later was tall, stooping, and completely hairless. His light grey suit was dandified and there was a bright flower in his buttonhole. His bored, almost vacant expression gave him the air of a well-bred *rentier*, but the air was false. He had been born in a Paris slum, and he worked very hard for his living. He was head of the department that dealt with the internal affairs of Soviet Russia. At the moment he was a very worried man.

As Miss Bond opened the door for him, he gave a fine bow to her and, preparing himself for martyrdom, walked into the stifling room.

"Ah, there you are, Igor. Come in and sit down." Kirk's hand, which lacked three fingers and was a mass of scar tissue, waved him to a seat. "Now what brings you here at this hour? Something important, I hope."

"I'm not sure, General, but I thought you should know about it at once." Trubenoff edged his chair out of the line of the huge fire. "I must say you keep things pretty warm in here."

"I certainly do, my boy. Can't stand the cold." There was a sudden glow of pride on Kirk's face. "Had that fire specially made for me, as it happens, and I'm quite delighted with it. First time I've felt really comfortable for years.

"And now, Igor, though I wouldn't describe myself as a busy man, I do have work to do. Just what was it you wanted to see me about? Urgent, I presume?"

"No, General, I would not call it urgent at the moment, but

I think you'll find it interesting." The Russian pulled a slim gold case from his pocket. The cigarettes it contained were oval Egyptians and carried his monogram tastefully picked out in green and gold.

"I'm afraid it's about those wretched creatures of the L.W.R. Something fresh has cropped up."

"Oh no, Igor, you surely don't mean to tell me you came up here just to talk about them. This really makes my day." Kirk groaned loudly, for the L.W.R., or League of White Russians, was a thorn in his side. It had started far back in the twenties; an organization of crackpot expatriates who had called themselves by Tzarist titles which no longer existed, and devoted their energies to such harmless activities as releasing balloons bearing political slogans whenever the wind was in the general direction of the Soviet Union.

Of late, however, the L.W.R. had become much more troublesome. Having received the backing of various influential figures in America and England, and an influx of new blood from Soviet deserters, it now claimed to be an important espionage group with a chain of adherents behind the Iron Curtain. The worst of it was that Sir Patrick Hay, the Minister of Foreign Affairs, recently elevated from Forests and Fisheries, had fallen under the spell of the L.W.R., and it had been made abundantly clear to Kirk that the department was to remain on civil terms with them. The memory of his last interview with Hay still annoyed Kirk considerably.

"No, General," Sir Patrick had said. "I can't say I'm pleased with the way things have been going of late, and in my view you need all the friends you can get." As always happened when Sir Patrick wanted to drive home a point, a rasp of Dublin had crept into his accent. "This fellow, Danilenko, now. As it happens I met him at Cowes last week, and was rather taken by him. Oh yes, a flamboyant chap maybe, like so many foreigners, but I think he might be useful to us, you know. It's not for me to tell you your business, of course, General, but I think your department should encourage him whenever possible." Sir Patrick had smiled in the most pleasant way as he spoke and patted Kirk's arm, but the threat was there all right. The department was to keep on friendly terms with the League of White Russians, and how they hated it.

"The L.W.R., Igor. You know those damned initials always make me think their monkey show is a railway company. I only wish it were." Kirk dragged hard on his cigar in irritation. "Well, what is it this time, old boy? The plans for another uprising in the Ukraine which will sweep the Bolsheviks away like chaff before the wind? The report of another rocket base in Poland which we know about already?"

"No, General, I'm afraid it's nothing as simple as that." Trubenoff pulled out a silk handkerchief and lightly stroked his forehead. "It's about old Tania Vitgeft. It seems that they've found the body at last."

"Have they indeed? And high time, too. Where was it, Igor? In Scotland or the north of England, I suppose?"

"No, sir, not in Scotland, and that's why I thought you should know at once. It seems that she never left her own house. The body was found in a trunk covered by books. The police say she had been dead for at least six months."

"I see. Yes, you were quite right to tell me this." Kirk's face was very thoughtful now, and his maimed hand drummed quietly on the desk.

"In her own house, eh? And that puts us in a very poor spot, doesn't it? A very poor spot indeed." He stared across the room and considered the life and disappearance of the late Princess Vitgeft. She hadn't been a real princess, of course. Trubenoff, whose knowledge of the Russian aristocracy was encyclopaedic, had been quite certain about that. Just a lady's maid who, in 1921, had escaped from Vladivostok taking her mistress's jewellery and credentials with her. For years she seemed to have wandered aimlessly about the world, and then finally settled in London where the L.W.R. had taken her to its bosom and paid her a small annuity.

Yes, Kirk remembered Tania Vitgeft, or whatever her real

name was, all right. A tall, gaunt, almost emaciated old woman who dressed in the fashions of another age: long black cloaks that brushed the ground, moth-eaten feather boas, toques with the mildew showing on them, and always a faint smell of mustiness. A power in the ranks of the League of White Russians, though. Whenever a Soviet citizen had deserted to the West, old Tania had gone rushing to the scene bearing pamphlets, demands for information he probably hadn't got, and offers to help rehabilitate him. The department hadn't really blamed the Soviet Intelligence service for wishing her dead.

"And her body was in that house for at least six months and the police never found her. Haven't the blighters even got noses?"

"I shouldn't think they bothered to look very closely, General." Trubenoff felt slightly sorry for his chief, for the inactivity of the police had been largely due to his advice. As far as Kirk was concerned, Tania Vitgeft had been abducted and killed by Soviet agents somewhere in Scotland and there was nothing to be done about it. The case was closed, and if amateurs wanted to play with fire they must take the consequences.

He recalled the details of her disappearance. Towards the end of January, two Russian seamen had deserted from a trawler off the Shetlands, and old Tania had hurried north to interview them. The same kind of thing had often happened before, but this time there was a slight difference. An hour before her train was due to leave an anonymous phone call had informed the department that Soviet agents were preparing to abduct her at the station. Kirk had derided the idea but, for the sake of the record, a plain-clothes man had been sent to King's Cross. In due course Vitgeft had been seen to arrive and board the train. There was no chance of any mistake either. Kirk's man had recognized that tall, flapping figure at first glance. He had watched the last of the coaches pull away from the platform and then gone home.

The rest of the story was quite clear, too. She had dined on the train, the waiters were quite clear about that, and she was alive after Newcastle. The car attendant had seen her standing in the corridor as though unable to sleep. But at Edinburgh, where friends were waiting to meet her—nothing. Not a trace of her. The train had stopped at Berwick, though, and she might have left it there. That was the theory that both the police and the department accepted. Which the department was glad to accept, for Tania Vitgeft had been like a gadfly to them for years, and they were delighted to be rid of her, whatever the L.W.R. had to say about lack of protection for its members. Once, in his cups, Trubenoff had silently toasted Comrade Peter Kun, head of Soviet Intelligence in Western Europe, for removing her.

"All the same, the fact that her body was found in her own house puts us on a very sticky wicket, General." During the week Trubenoff lived in an exotic Mayfair flat decorated like a stage set for a Chekhov play, but his week-ends were spent with a great tweedy cruiser of a woman whose address was The Old Manor House, Thornhanger, Marlborough; English sporting parlance thus came easily to him.

"Yes, it could do, but that's not what worries me at the moment." Kirk's voice was like the growl of an old, ill-tempered dog. "What I want to know is—why should they go to all this trouble?"

"Why? Sorry, but I'm not with you, sir. Revenge perhaps. To make an example of her which would put the fear of death into the others."

"No, no, you aren't with me, Igor. I don't mean why they should *want* to kill her, but why they did it in such a round-about way." Kirk pulled himself up from his chair and stared out of the window across the roofs of Southwark: endless traffic in the narrow streets, an electric sign flickering against the sunlight, and St. Paul's like a toy church on the far horizon.

"Oh, I can think of a dozen reasons why the M.V.D. might like to put old Tania out of the way, but why go to so much trouble over it? From what you've told me it seems clear that she was either brought back from Scotland, or killed in the house and somebody impersonated her on the train. Not a very difficult thing to do, perhaps, but why bother with a masquerade? Why not merely kill her in the house, or push her out of the sleeping car and have done with it? If they'd used an anonymous professional killer in either case we'd never have caught up with him.

"By the way, what was the cause of death?"

"She died of thirst, General." The Russian opened his briefcase and pulled out a slim green folder. "The body was found in a trunk, as I told you, and it had become mummified. She had received a heavy blow under the jaw, but it hadn't killed her. There are clear signs that she lived for some time in the trunk—probably for days. The lid was loose, and she would at least have had enough air to breathe.

"No, not a death I'd choose, sir." Trubenoff handed Kirk the police photographs and tried to imagine what it would have been like. The smell of old leather and heavy books pressing down on you. Old frail limbs struggling against the sides of the trunk and the pressure of the books, but in time you knew it was useless. A thin voice crying for help, but soon you knew that was useless too, for you lived quite alone and there was no one to hear you. Prayers might have come then, perhaps, with your finger-nails scratching against the cloth-lined walls of your prison. And, at last, nothing except pain and fear, though the little glimmer of light through the lid might have allowed you to distinguish night from day.

"Yes, that's true enough." Kirk stared at the photographs. "A very nasty death, carried out by somebody with a great deal of confidence and a most refined taste in cruelty. You know, I'm almost beginning to revise my ideas. This looks more like the work of a maniac than of the M.V.D.

"But just a minute, Igor. There's something else, isn't there—something you haven't told me." Kirk laid the photographs on the desk and looked at the Russian. "Come on, old boy, just cut out the secretive Slav act and tell me what else they found."

"I was just going to, General." With the air of a conjurer producing his final ace, Trubenoff handed him another photograph. It showed a section of the side of the trunk and there was a line of scratches across it. "If you look at that under a glass, I think you'll find it interesting."

"Thank you." Kirk laid the picture on his blotter and bent over it with a magnifying glass in his maimed hand. His face showed no expression at all as the scratches wavered and then turned to a line of writing.

"And she wrote this six months ago," he said very quietly. "'August the 8th M.K. arrives—M.K. will die.' And 'M.K.' can only refer to Michael Kapitza. No, it's impossible—quite impossible." He threw the glass away from him. "She couldn't have known he was coming. Why, the visit wasn't even definitely fixed till last June."

"All the same, General, I think we should assume that she may have known." Trubenoff stubbed out the cigarette and leaned far back in his chair, thinking of M.K., the man who was due to visit London on the eighth of the month. Michael Kapitza, the Russian statesman whom the whole Western world was waiting to welcome. Michael Kapitza, who was already second in command of the Supreme Soviet and seemed bound to succeed Khrushchev—a man who claimed that he had just one aim and one ambition in life: to tear down the barriers and live in peaceful coexistence with the West. A man with a lot of enemies, too. Trubenoff frowned slightly as he thought of them. Neither he nor Kirk was sure of the situation in Moscow, but it did seem that the Old Guard who hated Kapitza still held great power in the police and the armed forces and would not hesitate to use it if the opportunity arose.

"Yes, I think we should assume that she might have stumbled onto something, sir," he said. "That somehow she learned that Kapitza's visit was planned months back in Moscow, and at the same time learned that there is to be an attempt on his life over here—that she wrote it down before she died."

"And you think they would dare, Igor—you honestly think they would dare to try and kill him in London?"

"I think they might, General, because they daren't try anything against him in Russia without the risk of a civil war. By all accounts, the balance of power there is almost equally divided between friends and enemies of Kapitza.

"But look at it from their point of view. They know that if this visit is a success, there's nothing to stop Kapitza taking full control of the Soviet Government. They also know that as soon as that happens, a lot of heads will roll: Vladimir Skyrdoff's for example, Paula Stein's, Alex Chunkin's, Marshal Radenko's—to mention just a few of them. Yes, a great many people in Russia would like to kill Kapitza, and they may feel that this visit to London is a Heaven-sent chance to do it without risk to themselves."

"Yes, I suppose that's true." Once again Kirk glanced at the scrawled message in the photograph. "And so, for the time at least, we'll assume that old Tania didn't just write this in delirium, but that it means exactly what it seems to say. Kapitza's visit was planned before she died, and there is to be an attempt on his life over here.

"And the first thing we've got to do is to find out how she possibly could have known." He picked up the list of numbers that was beside the telephone.

"Yes, I'm afraid it's time we took Patrick Hay's advice for once and paid a call on the League of White Russians." Although he had found his number now, he didn't lift the phone at once. He stood smiling at Trubenoff.

"Yes, Igor, I'm afraid we'll have to do that. If Tania Vitgeft really did stumble on the truth, there is just one person who might be able to tell us more." His smile widened and he thrust forward his jaw in the manner of Mussolini. "That's right, old boy, Boris Grigoreyevich Danilenko—the Bogus Colonel, as you so aptly named him."

CHAPTER THREE

The building that housed the headquarters of the League of White Russians was part of a pleasant Regency terrace tucked away in a little cul-de-sac behind Knightsbridge. Its entrance hall was bare and cold and floored with black marble. There was a marble staircase winding gracefully upwards and, by the door, a marble bas-relief, showing a man's profile, stated that the house had once been the property of Sir Mortimer Jacques, philanthropist, man of letters, and inventor of the self-winding steam plough, 1805-1892. Beyond Sir Mortimer's chilly features was a painted board giving the names and occupations of the present tenants: "2nd Floor—Tupper & Athelstan, technical translation agents. 1st Floor—John Friendship Ltd., Publishers (Incorporating the Boileau Press)." No name for the Ground Floor, but a little flag device made up from a St. Andrew's Cross and the Two-Headed Eagle, with an arrow pointing to a door beside the stairs.

"Most impressive, if you like that sort of thing," Kirk said to Trubenoff, scowling at the plaque. They marched forward, their feet clicking on the marble. The door carried the same emblem, with the words "Knock and Enter" below it. Kirk gave a sharp rap and they walked in.

"Good morning, gentlemen." The room was very long and narrow, almost a passage, and a woman sat behind a desk at the end of it with two more doors at either side of her. She was middle-aged and comfortable looking, with loose grey hair, wide smiling eyes, and an old fawn jersey which had started to unravel slightly at the neck. She looked like a very nice unmarried aunt—a knitter of children's clothes, a sender of picture postcards, the welcome visitor at Christmas who never forgot anybody's present. Not at all the kind of person that Kirk had expected to see.

"Good morning, madam. My name is Kirk and this is my colleague, Mr. Trubenoff." He reached in his pocket and handed her a visiting card. "We have an appointment with Colonel Danilenko."

"With the Colonel! But this is very strange, I had no idea that he was seeing anybody this afternoon." She put on a pair of glasses and squinted suspiciously at the card, as though checking his authority to read a gas-meter. "General Charles Kirk," she said, frowning as she laid it down on the desk.

"Yes, this is all very strange, sir. Nobody told me that we were having any visitors today. Just whom did you make this appointment with, please?"

"I don't know his name, but I spoke to a man at your number about half an hour ago. He told me that it would be quite in order for us to call." Kirk flushed with impatience. He had no idea whether this woman was just an incompetent old busybody filled with the desire to preserve her employer's privacy, or whether Danilenko was playing hard to get.

"That is quite correct, Mary, I spoke to these gentlemen." The door to the left of the desk had opened and a man was smiling at them. In the gloom of the doorway he looked young and incredibly handsome, with high Slavonic cheekbones, a wave of blond hair sweeping over his forehead, and a slim, almost girlish body. It was only when he came into the light that they saw he was old—terribly old. The crown of hair was brittle with dye, the flesh was dry and wizened over the cheekbones, and the hand he held out to Kirk was as slim and white as a woman's.

"Good afternoon, General Kirk," he said. "My name is Gregor Baikal, and I once had the pleasure of meeting you before under rather more dramatic circumstances."

"I remember." Baikal's hand felt lifeless and his face reminded Kirk of trick Victorian engravings designed to show the impermanence of the flesh: a lovely smiling lady in the distance whose features changed to a grinning death mask when viewed at close quarters. Eight years ago Baikal had been a choreographer of the Leningrad Ballet and had asked for asylum while the company was in England. Like a good showman, he had made the scene impressive—a group of people filing through the customs shed at London Airport and then one man turning and running back towards the barrier. With the publicity that followed, there had been no question of not allowing him to stay.

"But you seem to have changed your occupation, Mr. Baikal," Kirk said, releasing the icy hand as soon as politeness allowed. "I thought you were still at Sadler's Wells."

"No, I left there a year ago, General. They were very kind to me, but I felt I wanted a more serious employment." The man's voice was a complete medley of accents and no one could have placed his nationality.

"But if you and your friend would be good enough to wait in the Colonel's office, I will tell him you are here." He opened a door to their right, bowing slightly as he did so, and then shut it behind them.

"Well, we can't deny that he doesn't do himself well, sir." Trubenoff stared around the enormous room which might have been a stage set for some Ruritanian palace. Two glittering chandeliers hung from the ceiling, the walls were lined with mirrors, and a pulpit-like desk, painted white and gold, stood against the far wall. The chair behind the desk bore the same cross and eagle device, and above it hung a life-size painting of the late Tzar and Tzarina. On either side of the picture were rows of photographs of officers in white uniforms, many of them with black bows tied to the frames.

"Yes, he does all right for himself, Igor. Much better than we poor blighters at the Ministry." Kirk's eyes took in everything, like a cat examining a new house. "But do you feel what I'm feeling, old boy?"

"That we're being watched, sir? Oh yes, and what's more, I think I know from where." Trubenoff crossed towards the desk and studied a big oval mirror. The glass had a sharp metallic look about it and, almost hidden by its curve, he could make out a tiny circle of pinpoints. "Yes, a look-through job all right, and what's more, I wouldn't be a bit surprised if there wasn't a tape-recorder or a microphone hidden away as well. We need rather a stronger term than *cloak-and-dagger* to describe this outfit, I think." The two men grinned at each other, and then turned as the door opened.

Colonel Boris Grigoryevich Danilenko didn't merely walk into the room. He clanked in like a traction engine, heavy feet pounding the carpet, bull head thrust forward, great gnarled hands clenched behind his back, three rows of plate-like medals jangling on his chest, and a very tight suit struggling to contain his seventeen stone of bone and muscle.

"So, you have come to me at last, gentlemen," he said, and his voice seemed to shake the entire room. "At last you realize that you need our help, and you have come to me cap in hand."

Kirk didn't answer him for a moment. The phrase *cap in hand* rankled considerably, and he counted five before replying, in the hope of keeping his temper. As he counted, he considered the Berlin Wall. If only it had been built sooner, he thought, if only the blighters had put it up ten years ago, then he would never have known this obnoxious person. Three days after the death of Stalin, Danilenko had put on a full dress uniform and, with his medals and epaulets clanking like a moving hardware store, had marched across the checkpoint into the British sector of the city. To the best of Kirk's knowledge, he had left the East because of a scandal regarding the wife of a Polish diplomat, but the press and the public didn't think that. "Colonel Freedom," they had hailed him, "The Hero of Stalingrad" who had seen the light. One Sunday newspaper had even compared him to a St. Paul having a blinding vision on some Muscovite road to Damascus.

But whatever the truth, Danilenko was a person to be reckoned with now. Head of the L.W.R., with this imposing office, a country house near Dorking, and a white Rolls-Bentley with his monogram on the doors. He also had the ear of several important public figures, including Sir Patrick Hay, Kirk's bugbear.

"No, Colonel, I have not come to you cap in hand," Kirk said coldly. "I have come because I think it possible that your organization may have been withholding certain information from us—information which it was your clear duty to give us."

"Our duty, General Kirk! You say *our* duty?" The Russian lowered his bulk against the corner of the desk, and his hand ran across the rows of medals, as though to adjust their hang. He had put them on both to impress his visitors and as an excuse to keep them waiting.

"But what about your duty, gentlemen? What about Princess Vitgeft, whose life it was your duty to protect—whose death you seemed to think quite unimportant till today? No, you never worried about that, did you? You merely thought she was an interfering busybody, and were doubtless quite pleased when the M.V.D. murdered her. And I wonder if you think I'm just a busybody, you know. Even after the affair of George Vane, I wonder that." He mentioned the name of a British physicist who had been preparing to flee to Russia, but at the last moment had been arrested on information received from the L.W.R.

"No, I don't think you are a busybody, Colonel." Kirk spoke the truth, for the words he would actually have used to describe Danilenko were *boor*, *braggart* and *confidence trickster*. In his opinion, the evidence against Vane had been stumbled on by chance, and he considered the L.W.R. to be a bunch of parasites who took money from the British Government under false pretences. All the same, he remembered those tell-tale scratches on the side of the trunk in which Tania Vitgeft had died. If he was to know the truth about them, he would have to be nice to Danilenko. He forced his face into a smile.

"But can't we forget old differences now, Colonel?" he said. "As I told your Mr. Baikal on the telephone, this matter is extremely important. If there is to be an attack on Kapitza while he is in this country, it is up to both our organizations to stop it. Don't you think that it is time we worked together?"

"To work together!" For a long moment Danilenko stared

at them without speaking and both Kirk and Trubenoff could see injured dignity and pleasure fighting in his face. Then, almost without warning, his expression changed to a great wide beam of delight. He reached forward and took Kirk's hand in a bone-crushing grip.

"Yes, of course we can work together," he said. "That is what I have wanted for years—what I have wanted more than anything in the world. But do please sit down, gentlemen." He waved them to chairs and sat down behind his desk.

"Yes, we shall work together at last and I and my organization are at your complete disposal. If there is any way in which we can help, you have only to ask." His smile flickered from Kirk to Trubenoff.

"But tell me something please, sir. Your name was once quite a famous one in Russia. Are you by any chance a relative of Admiral Gniaz Trubenoff who commanded a Black Sea squadron during the First World War?"

"He was my father, but it is unimportant." Coming from Danilenko, Trubenoff found the reference distasteful.

"Ah, but it is important to me, you know." The big man craned forward across his desk. "To me everything about our friends in the British Intelligence Service is important. You know, General Kirk, for instance, I have made quite a study of you. I know all your career from Sandhurst to the present day; your hobbies—grouse shooting is the most important, is it not?; your likes and dislikes—by the way, I hope this room is warm enough for your comfort; how you had the misfortune to damage your hand at the second battle of Ypres—"

"Never mind about my hand, Colonel." Kirk struggled to contain his annoyance. "This business is serious and the sooner we get down to work the better. Here are the photographs I discussed with your assistant on the telephone."

"Thank you." Danilenko laid the first picture on his desk and switched on a lamp. "Yes, yes, I see," he said, and there was no smile on his face now. "Yes, I quite understand why you should want to see me, gentlemen. M.K. Somebody named

M.K. who arrives on the eighth of this month. Somebody who dies that day. And Tania wrote this just before she was killed. Is there nothing more you can tell me, General Kirk?"

"No, that's all we have to go on, I'm afraid. The house was thoroughly searched after they found the body, but nothing of any significance came to light. I think we can guess whom she meant by *M.K.*, though."

"Guess! I don't have to guess. M.K. is Michael Kapitza." The Colonel pushed the first picture to one side and looked at the other. "And somehow Tania learned that he was intending to come to England long before it was officially announced. She also learned that they intend to kill him.

"Oh you silly, vain old bitch." He muttered the words aloud. "Why didn't you tell me? You got onto something, but you tried to be clever and keep it to yourself till you were quite sure. And before you were sure, before you had all your facts, somebody caught up with you." He shook his head over the face of the dead lady's maid who had posed as a princess for forty years.

"No, General, I can't tell you how she found out about this. Though Tania was my friend, I would be the last person to pretend she was entirely sane. She liked secrecy—keeping things to herself till she was really certain—even the title *Princess* was just a sham. She was only a servant till she left Russia. She enjoyed playing games, in fact." Danilenko got up from the desk and stared at a big map of Soviet Russia and its satellite countries that was pinned to the door. It seemed to be about the only functional object in the huge ornate room. He looked much older as he stood before it and all the bounce left him.

"I can tell you one thing, though. To the best of my belief this message is the exact truth. They are going to try and kill Kapitza, though *liquidate* is the expression they would use, but they cannot kill him anywhere here." His hand waved across the map like a geography teacher explaining a point to his class.

"Oh, I know what I'm talking about, gentlemen. Before I changed my views, I was one of these people myself, one of the Old Guard, the old unrelenting Bolsheviks who want to hang on to power whatever it costs them. Many of them died, of course: Stalin in his bed, Beria with three bullets in his guts, Lynov screaming. . . . But there are still plenty of them left and this Kapitza is the man who will send them packing. If you were in their position, wouldn't you try to kill him, General Kirk?"

"Yes, I think I'd try to kill him, Colonel." Kirk considered the man who was coming, and a score of photographs ran through his head. Kapitza standing at the saluting base in the Red Square. Kapitza before the United Nations. Kapitza with his arm round the shoulders of a spaceman. A strangely liberal face, for all the uniform collar that tilted his chin upwards and the little goatee beard worn in honour of Lenin. Kapitza had started as a fanatic, working his gun at Tzaritzin till it had jammed with heat, but he had changed with the years and now seemed to want nothing but peace and friendship with the West. If ever he gained full power in Russia, most of the world would sleep sounder in its bed and a lot of jobs would change hands in Moscow.

"Yes, I'd have a shot at killing him," he said. "And you're quite right, of course. They couldn't risk an attempt in the Soviet Union. He's so popular at the moment that there'd be strikes and riots from one end of the country to the other.

"And so they'll try it here. Then, if they succeed, there'll be no repercussions at all. It will be put down as the work of some mad fanatic with a pathological hatred of all Russian statesmen. Someone belonging to an organization very much like your own, in fact."

"Like us!" Danilenko raised his eyebrows. "But, gentlemen, Kapitza is the one man on whom we are pinning our hopes. If he controlled Russia we would see the first real break in the Curtain, and that is what we are working for. My organization wants to protect him even more than you do."

"I know that, Colonel. I was merely stating the kind of story they would circulate if he were to die in England. Yes, we both want to protect Kapitza, but how much chance have we got, unless we know much more?" Kirk leaned back, tapping his mutilated hand on the arm of his chair, and considered how it might be.

Kapitza was coming by sea from Leningrad. At Southend he would transfer from his cruiser to a naval launch which would take him to Westminster Steps, where he was to be met by the Prime Minister and other dignitaries. On the surface the security arrangements were complete. The Thames bridges would be cleared of the public during his journey up-stream, and he would be surrounded by a squad of plain-clothes men, English and Russian. He was to stay at the White Lodge in Richmond Park and there would be a three-mile cordon around it.

Yes, on the surface, Kapitza looked safe enough, but only on the surface. Even as he sat there Kirk seemed to see a window opening very slowly to show the telescopic sights of a rifle behind it. Unless they had much more information to go on, they just couldn't guarantee his safety.

"And that's why we've come to see you, Colonel," he said. "If we're to stand a chance of protecting Kapitza, we've got to know the details of the plot to kill him. I was hoping that Tania Vitgeft might have confided in you, but it seems I was wrong. All the same, you may still be able to help us. Can you give me any idea as to where she could have got her information?"

"No, not yet, but I shall find out for you." Danilenko stood back from the map, so that they could see it better. Here and there it was dotted with little white flags.

"General Kirk," he said, and some of the old hostility had returned to his voice. "We have not been good friends in the past, you and I. You have often sneered at our organization. Cloak-and-Dagger Clowns, League of White Rabbits, are some of the terms you have used to describe us, I think. Colonel Bogus, eh, Mr. Trubenoff? Even after the affair of George Vane you said things like that.

"Well, that's all forgotten and we are friends. All the same, it will give me pleasure to show you both how good we really are." Once again his hand ran across the map.

"These flags are the locations of our members in Soviet-controlled territory, and not one of them is merely a paid agent, but a truly dedicated human being who is quite prepared to die for our cause if need be." There was a sudden glow of pride in his face as he spoke.

"And, if need be, they *will* die, General. You want to know how Tania got her information, but I will do better than that. If there is a plot to kill Kapitza when he arrives in London, you will be told about it. Even if it means destroying our whole movement, you will get the facts in time to stop it." The Colonel turned away from the map. He didn't sit down at his desk, but stared up at the big oil painting of the Tzar and Tzarina. There was an ornamental sword hanging below the frame; he lifted it down and pointed with the blade.

"Nicholas the Second, Tzar of all the Russias," he said, and he might have been talking to himself. The sword swung lower to the photographs beside the picture.

"Alexander Vasilievich Kolchak and Anton Denikin, the last loyalist commanders to stand on Russian soil. They failed, didn't they, gentlemen? They failed because they were too weak.

"Well, nobody is going to say that Boris Danilenko is weak—not after August the eighth." The pride in his face was like a great shining lamp. Kirk's opinion of Danilenko began to alter. Until a few moments ago he had thought of him as a strutting, self-important clown, but quite suddenly he seemed to know that the man really was effective. Every inch of his big, clumsy body was effective, in spite of the theatrical manner, the jangling medals, and his silly sword.

CHAPTER FOUR

"No, General, there's no chance of postponing Kapitza's visit at this stage. I'm also afraid that if anything happened to him while he is in this country, you would be the obvious scape-goat." Martin Wilde, first secretary to the Minister, fiddled with a blackened briar pipe on his desk. He had known Kirk for years and respected him deeply, but at the moment was begin-ning to feel that he was quite unnecessarily worried.

"Yes, if anything went wrong, you would be held respon-sible. I'm beginning to know our new master, Patrick Hay, rather well now, and I think he'd throw you to the wolves without a word in your defence. But after all, what can go wrong, General? Surely your security arrangements will be up to scratch."

"They'll be as thorough as we can make them, Mr. Wilde, but without more information I'm still not satisfied." Kirk pulled at his cigar, once again going over the arrangements he had made with the police and the Russian Embassy: the launch coming up river under the deserted bridges, the cor-doned park, and the squad of plain-clothes men who would surround Kapitza wherever he went. He knew they were all quite inadequate.

"We'll do all we can to protect him, of course, but it's not enough. Oh, we can deal with any private individual who tries to put a bullet into him—any nut who imagines he has a mis-sion to wipe out the Soviet hierarchy—but if there has been a serious attempt planned in Moscow, then I've got to know more about it before we can guarantee his safety.

"Look at it from our point of view and remember what happened at Sarajevo in 1914. There were at least six would-be assassins stationed in the city to try and kill the Archduke Francis Ferdinand, and though five of them failed, Gavrilo Prinsip got him in the end. Weapons have improved a lot since those days, you know." Once again Kirk seemed to see that slowly opening window and the glint of telescopic sights behind it.

"Yes, I know all that, General." Wilde's hand trembled slightly as he fondled the pipe. He was trying to stop smoking and the very feel of it was torture to him. The clouds of cigar smoke from Kirk's side of the desk did nothing to relieve his craving.

"I also agree with you that there are many influential people in Russia who would like to see Kapitza out of the way. No, I'm certainly not denying that. But what real evidence have we that they're intending to make an attempt on his life over here? All you've got to go on is this scribbled message written by a dying woman who was most probably delirious. From the report you've just shown me, her death looks more like the work of a maniac than a political killing." Temptation suddenly became too strong for Wilde and he started to ram tobacco into the pipe. He felt ten years younger as he did so.

"Good God, General, you're surely not telling me that you put any faith in these crackpots of the League of White Russians? Whatever Hay may feel about them, I would have thought that you would see through them. League of White Russians indeed! Pack of lunatics, if you ask me. I hear that they've even set up a pretender to the throne now. A poor old boy of eighty-five called the Grand Duke Alexis who just wants to sleep his life quietly away on a Biarritz beach. They make me sick."

"Yes, I know how you feel all right." Usually Kirk respected Wilde's opinions and until a few hours ago he would have heartily agreed with him. All the same, the date given in that scratched message was too clear for comfort. In his mind's eye he could see the launch coming up London River with a little bearded man standing on her bridge. Then, unless he could forestall it, a gun would be raised in the far distance and Kapitza would go down. The future of mankind would be much greyer from that moment and his own future would cease to exist. Disgrace, dismissal, the headlines in the papers and afterwards . . . ? Long arid years of enforced retirement seemed to stretch in front of him. Gloomy rooms in Bath, Cheltenham, or Eastbourne; rounds of golf in the mornings, heavy overcooked meals, and a game of billiards with the marker before going to bed. Already he could hear the whispered conversations from the hotel bar—"Somebody once, but they sacked him. Just a has-been now." Click—click—click ran the sound of billiard balls in his head. If Michael Kapitza was to die, he would almost be dying himself.

"But it's the date that bothers me, Mr. Wilde," he said. "Tania Vitgeft died last January. Unless she had some very reliable information from Russia, how could she possibly know that Kapitza was due to arrive here on August the eighth? I understand that his visit wasn't even confirmed till eight weeks ago."

"Well, I suppose there could have been a security leak about his first visit." Wilde's voice was almost indifferent. He struck a match and held it over the pipe.

"The first visit! Just what do you mean?" Kirk's head jerked backwards as though Wilde had struck him. "Is there something I wasn't told about?"

"I've no idea whether you were told or not, General. It seemed quite unimportant at the time, though it may help to put your mind at rest now." The pipe was drawing to Wilde's full satisfaction and he spoke like a man at peace with the world.

"The fact is that well over eighteen months ago the Soviet Embassy approached us about a visit from Kapitza. There was nothing definitely settled, though August the eighth was suggested as the date of arrival. It seems that that's his wife's birthday and he wanted it in her honour. A nice example of the sentimental Slav for you—the soft childlike heart beating under the armour.

"At any rate it all came to nothing. As you remember,

Kapitza was laid up for some time—yes, appendicitis I think it was—and the visit was postponed. Then, eight weeks ago, they approached us again, and the same date, August the eighth, was asked for."

"So, that was it." Kirk leaned far back in his chair, and, though he was furious that the department had not been informed about the first visit, he felt as though a huge weight had been lifted from his shoulders.

Yes, that was it all right. Old Tania Vitgeft had stumbled on the truth, but she was a year behind—a whole damned year. He smiled at Wilde through a haze of smoke, and he saw quite clearly how it must have been. Michael Kapitza had planned his trip to London, but before it was even confirmed, he had learned that there was to be an attack on his life. The excuse of ill-health, a period in a nursing home, and apologies to the British Government would have seemed the obvious course, while his police hunted down the would-be assassins or, what was more important, the people who employed them.

And then, over a year later, when he knew that his enemies were dead or powerless, that sentimental man with a fondness for celebrating his wife's birthday had decided to ask for another invitation.

"Well, Mr. Wilde, if your people had had the courtesy to tell us about this at the beginning, you'd have saved me a very bad headache." Kirk grumbled on principle, but he felt nothing but relief. Tania Vitgeft had somehow learned the truth about that first visit and it had stuck in her mind like an obsession. Then, months later, in the musty prison of the trunk, it had come bubbling out, and her weakening fingers had scratched a warning. A warning which was quite meaningless, for it referred to an event that had already been forestalled.

Who had killed her? He would like to know that, of course, but it was a job for the police, not the department. All that need concern him was Kapitza's safety while he was in England, and there was no need to worry any more. The assassins had been taken care of in Russia and that seemed assured.

"I'm sorry you weren't informed, General, but all's well that ends well, eh?" Wilde closed the folder on Tania Vitgeft and slid it across the desk. "And now let me get you a glass of sherry." He got up and crossed to what looked like a quite genuine Jacobean spinet that stood in the corner of his office. At the touch of a switch the keyboard slid aside to reveal a shining array of bottles and glasses.

"By the way, have you heard about our masters' last piece of brilliance? That's right, the East African business. It seems that they've committed themselves to both sides, and haven't a clue how to get out of it." He laid two glasses on the desk, and with all thoughts of Kapitza and Tania Vitgeft far out of their minds, they began to discuss the folly of professional politicians.

CHAPTER FIVE

But though Kirk might have dismissed Tania Vitgeft's warning from his mind, Boris Danilenko was still quite certain that Kapitza was to die and he was on his way to find out how.

He leaned against the rail of the cross-channel streamer *King Leopold I*, watching the flat Belgian coastline creep into the horizon. He was dressed in the brown habit of a monk, tied around his bulk with a white cord, while a cowl hid most of his face. His passport stated that he was Father Boris Parmen, Community of the Redemption, and he had letters in his pack to show that he had recently returned from mission work near Durban and was on his way to East Germany, where he had been invited to lecture on the South African Government's Apartheid policy. He made a slightly sinister figure as he stood there, a brooding, Slavonic Friar Tuck, with his huge feet straining against the open sandals and the staff in his hand looking more like a weapon than a means of support.

"Yes, Michael, just ten more hours and I should know how they intend to kill you." The forward deck was almost

deserted and he muttered the words aloud against the whine
of the engines as the ship shuddered, swung round, and began
to back into Ostend harbour; the fishermen on the piers
barely looking up as she passed. Whatever Kirk might have
told him about that earlier postponed visit of Kapitza's, Danilenko knew that his death was planned, for there were people
in Moscow who couldn't afford to let him live. All of the Old
Guard who were left—Skyrdoff, Radenko, Chunkin—knew
that their days were numbered if he ever stood at the head of
the Supreme Soviet, and they also knew that they couldn't kill
him in Russia. The attempt on Kapitza's life would be made
in London, and it was up to him, Boris Danilenko, to find out
exactly how they intended to go about it.

"Attention please. Will all passengers have their green landing cards ready." Wheezing and indistinct, the loudspeakers
made the announcement in French, Flemish, German, and
English, and the ship lurched against the side of the pier.
Meekly, as befitted his calling, Fr. Parmen, C.R., took his place
at the end of the queue and moved down the gangway into
Belgium.

And this really was a horrible town, he decided, staring
through his cowl at the square before the station. Stands selling shellfish and comic hats, a line of shabby open vehicles
drawn by small dispirited horses waiting for custom, and
everywhere buses, enormous gleaming buses with destination boards naming every corner of Europe and travel-weary
tourists being prodded aboard them like cattle into pens.
"Costa Brava Tour . . . Italian Lakes Tour . . . Blue Sky Tours
. . . Jackson's Tours . . . See Europe from an Armchair"—this
last seemed to be overdue in starting and was full of red-faced
ladies already fast asleep in their armchairs.

But it would be worse when the season got going later in
the month, he decided, much worse. Though he had been
born in a shack outside Minsk, Danilenko was a snob. He
scowled as he walked along the crowded front with the smell
of the sour sea mingling with closely packed humanity, fish

and chips, and diesel fumes. From every building neon signs and placards urged the British holiday-maker to buy and feel at home. "The Winston Churchill Bar . . . The Alexander Bar . . . The General Monté Grill and Restaurant—Steak and Chips and Mum's Apple Pie our Specialities . . . Genuine bargains in head-scarves, watches, half the price of home, novelty cards for your friends, genuine leather handbags, bikinis." Under the awning of a corner café, the Manchester Arms, a group of teenagers sat silently chewing bubble gum with the intensity of sleepwalkers. He hurried past them and turned down a quieter street away from the front with his staff tapping the pavement before him.

The Green Hat Club stood far back from the sea and the crowds in a little shabby square and looked as though it might once have seen better days a long time ago. Three letters of its electric sign had ceased to work, the paint was peeling from the façade, and the beaded curtains across the doorway had a sad brittle look as though they would fall apart at any moment. The uniformed barker at the door was fast asleep on a bench and didn't stir as Danilenko walked past him. Doubtless trade was very quiet in the morning, though a poster beside him announced the personal appearance of "La Belle Marie," once the pride of King Farouk's harem. Danilenko pushed through the curtain, pausing in the passage for a moment to let his eyes grow accustomed to the gloom, and then marched forward.

The place was just as he remembered it from three years back, though, if anything, a little more down at heel. There was a zinc-covered bar at the end of the room with the Union Jack and the Stars and Stripes draped above it, and a dais with a piano to the side. In the centre was a tiny dance floor and it seemed as if La Belle Marie had just finished her turn, for an ageing woman with a set simian smile and a spray of ostrich leathers attached to her backside was hurrying off amid desultory applause.

The few customers in the room sat squarely at their tables with mugs of warm, flat London beer at their side. Most of them looked like small shopkeepers or artisans. Those with women beside them seemed dispirited and ill at ease, but the majority, released by shopping wives to have a pint or two with old Harry, or Bill, or Len, were obviously having a wow of a time. Danilenko could imagine their reminiscences to work-mates back home: "Eh, you want to try it one day, lad. Little place in a back street there was, and a fat old lass danced about with nowt but a bunch o' feathers on 'er tail." As he entered the room one or two of them looked up at him with inter-est, obviously thinking he was another turn. The comic monk who would sing a vulgar song or dance a jig with suitable ges-tures in the right passages. They bent over their beer again when Danilenko ignored them and walked to the bar.

"Bonjour, mon père." The woman behind the counter was dressed completely in black and, though middle-aged now, her face looked as if it had once been very lovely. One side of it could have been, that is. The other, partly screened by a long lock of grey hair, was a nightmare. A child's horror with the flesh grey and withered and a great purple swelling hanging from the cheek like a living creature that had attached itself there.

"You are collecting for the poor, I suppose, mon père?" She barely looked up at Danilenko from the glass she was polish-ing, and there was no interest in her voice.

"Yes, madame, for the poor, as always." As Danilenko answered her, a ripple of excitement ran across the room and a stout red-faced gentleman wearing a comic cap climbed uncer-tainly up the dais to the piano. He looked hot and embarrassed and had obviously been urged on by his friends, but received a much better reception than La Belle Marie had done. "Come on, Harry boy, you show 'em what real music is now. Good old Harry, he's got what it takes." Cheers, applause, and raucous singing broke out as the aged machine burst into a surpris-ingly noisy rendering of a north country folk-song.

"But for which poor, mon père? There are many of them I think." The woman was forced to raise her voice slightly as her clientele put all they'd got into the song, but she still didn't look up from the glass. "For the poor of the North or of the South?"

"For neither, as it happens, madame. I am collecting for the poor of the East." Danilenko leaned forward towards her, keeping his eyes away from that terrible scar. "I have heard that the birds are flying early this year and it will be a hard winter."

"Yes, I have heard that, too. They will be flying high and early." As though the glass was at last cleaned to her full satisfaction, she put it down and motioned to the waiter to take her place behind the bar.

"And will you come with me, mon père, so that we can discuss my contribution to your fund." She lifted the flap of the counter and Danilenko followed her through it into a gloomy little room that lay behind.

"You baby, Boris, you great big silly baby." The woman closed the door and grinned at him. "Was there any need for all that rigmarole? I recognized you as soon as you came in in spite of that silly disguise. 'The birds are flying high and early' indeed! You really love it, don't you, Boris?"

"No, I don't love it, Rima, but perhaps it amuses me slightly." Danilenko slipped off his cowl and smiled back at her. "Also it seems necessary, you know. There may very well be one of our friends in the club now."

"In here! Among these cattle." She shook her head towards the faint strains of song that penetrated the door. "Don't make me laugh, old friend. My man at the door may appear to be asleep, but he would have woken up very quickly if anybody had followed you in.

"No, you are quite safe in this rat hole, and though I know you are in a hurry as always, you will still have a drink with me before we talk business. Oh yes, I insist, Boris. Your train doesn't leave for an hour, and there is plenty of time." She poured out two glasses and sat down at the table beside him. She was careful to keep one side of her face well in the shadow as she did so.

"Besides, you liked to drink with me once, Boris. Remember how it was in the old days with Peter and Shura. Yes, a long time ago—before the bear."

"But I still like drinking with you, Rima. Your very good health, my dear." Danilenko raised his glass to her and, as he did so, the years seemed to peel away and what had happened was as clear as yesterday. A hunting trip in the Urals when they were students. He and Shura and Rima and Peter Ravin. The long nights under the canvas when each tent seemed to be a little private world. The clear, clear mornings with the smell of snow coming down from the mountains and the camp fire shimmering in the air. The hot afternoons with sunlight mottling the Siberian plains that stretched all the way to the Pacific. And in the evening—horror.

No, he would never forget that evening. She and Peter had been walking a little way ahead of them up the slope with their arms around each other when it happened. A great grey figure rearing up like a man from behind the boulders to smash Peter's rifle to scrap-iron and sending him reeling down the path. He, Boris, had killed the bear with his first shot, but he wasn't quick enough. Before he could fire, its claws had reached out and torn half of Rima's face away.

Still there was no point in thinking of that now. The past was as dead as the bear and only the future mattered. He'd married Shura when he got his commission and she'd left him three years later, gently coughing her life away in the Gorki Clinic at Leningrad. Peter Ravin was buried under the rubble of Stalingrad, and only he and Rima remained now, exiles in the West since Stalin died, she running this club which was a clearing house for their agents, and he...? Well, at the moment, he was just a creature with one purpose and mission in life: to find out exactly how a man named Michael Kapitza was to die. Through the door the strains of "Blaydon Races" rose in crescendo: "There was lots of stands and monkey shows, and auld wives sellin' cider—"

"Yes, monkey shows, Boris, monkey shows is right. Just how long do we have to keep up this carnival, my dear?"

"As long as it takes us to complete the job, Rima." Danilenko finished his drink and pushed the glass away from him.

"And now let's talk business, please. I want to leave in ten minutes and must be sure that everything is arranged."

"As you wish." She opened a drawer and pulled out a heavy old-fashioned ledger. It appeared to contain a statement of the club's expenses, but one or two entries might have puzzled an accountant.

"And everything has been arranged, Boris, though it's a terrible risk you're going to take. Whatever this General Kirk may say, these people are efficient. Your train arrives at Berlin at eight o'clock this evening. The man who has the information you need will be waiting for you at nine sharp.

"No, there is no address, and he will contact *you*. Apparently he likes playing toy spies as much as you do yourself. All you have to do is to be at the Leipziger-strasse checkpoint at nine o'clock. Now, may I see your right hand, please?" She nodded as he laid it before her and closed the book.

"Yes, all quite correct and according to instructions, though I still think you're mad to go across the border yourself. Couldn't you have sent someone else, Boris? You're still well-known, and even with that disguise they may spot you at the checkpoint. And if they do—"

"If they do, then somebody else will have to take over from me." Danilenko stood up and pulled back his cowl. "No, I know the risk, Rima, but I have to speak to that man in Berlin personally. I have to know exactly how they intend to kill Kapitza. And now, goodbye, and thanks for passing on the message."

With a slightly rough and embarrassed gesture he bent down and kissed her hand. Then without another word he turned and went out of the door.

"Goodbye, Boris." The woman sat quite still at the table as the door closed behind him and there was a hint of tears in her eyes. "And please be careful. For my sake be careful, because we might have been good for each other once, after Peter and

Shura died. If only—" Her fingers ran across the swelling on her cheek and, though she was quite alone, she didn't seem to be talking to herself.

"Yes, we might have been good for each other, Boris. Big rough Boris Danilenko. As rough as the bear that stole my pretty face. Goodbye, Boris." She got up and moved to a telephone in the corner of the desk and she looked very tired and ill as she dialled a number. Her caller was no farther away than Brussels, but he would make a second call, and somebody else a third. Before Danilenko's train even reached Berlin, several people in Moscow would be informed of his visit.

CHAPTER SIX

It had been hot enough at Ostend and in the train which had carried him across Germany, but Berlin itself was stifling. Danilenko leaned far back against the cushions of the taxi. Under his thick habit his body felt like a grey cinder drained by heat and hunger. He had counted on eating on the train, but the dining car had been removed at the frontier, and there was no time to get a snack now. They had been twenty minutes late at Charlottenburg Station and Rima Elvoutzig had told him that he must be at the checkpoint at nine sharp. He cursed his stupidity for not buying sandwiches and stared gloomily out of the cab window.

The journey itself had been horrible. For the sake of appearances he had travelled second class and shared a compartment with a large and talkative family who had forced their unwelcome attentions on him from the start. The father, earnest, bald, and bespectacled, had bowed, clicked his heels, and announced with ceremony that his name was Braun and he was a *Meister*, whatever that might mean, at the Volkswagen at Wolfsburg. The three children had giggled incessantly and tried to outstare him, but the mother was the worst of all; an enormous blonde *Frau* who, whenever the train passed a place of interest, had squealed in praise of the Fatherland's beauties with cries of "Schön! Wie schön! Ach Gott, wie schön!" On three occasions she had dared to clutch him by the sleeve and almost drag him to the window as a dank wood, a ruined castle, and a grey, sluggish river slid by, screaming, "Pater, kom gleich, das ist so schön!" Mercifully they had left the train at the border, but his dislike of the German people had grown considerably during those few hours.

And Berlin had changed since he had last seen it. He looked with interest at the new buildings on the Kurfürstendam. Gleaming white concrete replacing the war-scarred brick, bright shops and cafés with shrubs and gay awnings before them, but at the end of the street, by the Zoo underground station, one familiar landmark—the broken shell of the Kaiser Wilhelm Memorial Church still preserved as a monument to pain; with its shattered spires standing out like Gothic ruins under the heavy sky.

Yes, a shining new city, but a dying city, too. The streets seemed much emptier than he remembered, and though the people looked gay, he sensed that it was a very surface gaiety. By now every one of them must know that they were living in a doomed world, shut in by the grey sky, and the wall which was doing its work well. A people who had only one hope left: if Michael Kapitza were to live, that wall might come down.

He was almost there now. Budapesterstrasse, Lutzostrasse, with the green of the Tiergarten to the north, and an acid tang of rubble rising from the ruins of the east. There was suddenly sweat on his forehead, but he wouldn't admit fear, even to himself. He just hoped that there hadn't been any mistake. If there had been, both he and the cause he served would be finished.

"Potsdamerplatz." The driver brought the cab to a halt, and leaned back to open the door. There was no curiosity or interest in his face as Danilenko paid him. The sight of a habited monk preparing to enter Communist-held territory might have been an everyday occurrence to him. In that doomed, divided city he had seen too much to register any more surprise.

But this was it. This was the same square he had walked across ten years ago. He had been a very different figure then with his uniform and his scarlet epaulets and his rows of medals jingling before him, and he just prayed that his present disguise was adequate. He pulled the cowl a little tighter over his head and walked slowly towards the sign that marked the end of the British sector. Beside it stood three German police and a British army sergeant with rifles slung over their shoulders, and beyond them was the wall. It looked much smaller and less impressive than he had imagined. Unmortared concrete blocks piled together as though they had been stacked in preparation for some routine building operation.

"Your papers please, sir." The first German policeman took his passport, glanced briefly at the cover, and then handed it to the British soldier who flicked it open and stared at the photograph. "Father Boris Parmen, C.R.," he read. Yes, he'd heard a good deal about the Community of the Redemption and disliked most of it. A bunch of troublemakers who wandered about the world stirring up unrest which people like himself had to sort out later. Well, if this imbecile wanted to go across the border he had no right to stop him. If he got himself locked up or even killed, so much the better.

"You understand that once you pass this point the West German and British Governments will no longer hold themselves responsible for your safety?" He gave the routine warning quite automatically, noting the number of the passport as he did so, and then handed it back to Danilenko. "Very well, you are free to go."

The wall ran straight across the end of the square with a gap where Leipzigerstrasse joined it. Beside the gap was a moveable barrier of barbed wire, drawn back at the moment, and behind the barrier a wooden hut with a notice that read, "YOU ARE NOW ENTERING THE DEMOCRATIC SECTOR OF BERLIN."

Danilenko walked slowly towards the three figures that lounged beside the hut. He made his steps drag slightly on the cobbles and leaned on his staff—the humble monk replacing the strutting colonel who had marched down this road ten years ago and now was going back. The men in front of him looked very smart in their blue uniforms of the People's Police, but their faces were tired and bored, as though they had been too long on duty.

"Passport." The lieutenant in charge of the checkpoint was very young and, though he might have been curious about Danilenko's dress, he didn't show it. His business was to stop people leaving the East Sector, not entering it.

"Thank you." He flicked the book open and glanced at the picture. "Would you please bare your head for a moment?"

"But certainly." Danilenko slipped back his cowl and smiled at him, though he didn't feel like smiling at all. The time was exactly nine o'clock and Rima had promised that there would be one of their members to meet him at the checkpoint. She had never let him down before, but this boy was obviously just a petty official carrying out a dull and routine assignment.

"I am afraid it is not a very good likeness," he said, "but passport photographs rarely are."

"So I hear—several times a day." There was no answering smile on the lieutenant's face. "Still, yours is at least recognizable." He pulled a notebook from his tunic and began to write down Danilenko's particulars. "Your name is Boris Parmen and you were born in Tallinn, but are now a British subject. What is your purpose in visiting the East German People's Republic, and how long do you intend to stay?"

"Just one night. I have been invited to address the senate of the university in the morning on the subject of racial discrimination in South Africa. I hope to start back to England as soon as I have given my lecture." He started to fumble in his pack. "I have a letter from Professor Comrade Litmann of the university which you might care to look at."

"No, I don't think that will be necessary." The boy pushed away his book and brought out a rubber stamp. "A very short visit, I'm afraid, but I hope that your lecture will be a great success." The stamp came down on the passport and he handed it back to Danilenko with a little formal bow.

"And that is all?" Danilenko felt completely at a loss. His enemies had not recognized him at the barrier, but neither had his friends. He started to move forward into East Berlin when another voice broke out at his side.

"No, no, that is not all—not quite all." The voice was thick and muddy, and its owner looked just like it. He stood in the doorway of the hut blinking slightly in the fading daylight. A fat little man with beads of sweat glistening on his forehead and a huge swollen belly lunging out like a sack before him. On the surface his face was kindly and rather stupid, but his eyes were very bright and hard. As Danilenko turned towards him his own eyes fell on the figures of the British and West German police across the square. They were no more than forty yards away, but it might have been a hundred miles. He knew what this man was. There was M.V.D., Soviet Intelligence Service, written on every bulge of that swollen little body.

"Yes, I thought I heard you say Tallinn just now, Comrade Lieutenant. Tallinn, Estonia, the capital of one of our loyal and devoted allies, I seem to remember. In view of that, I think I should have a word with our friend. Will you come into the hut for a moment, *Father*?" He grinned widely as though the title amused him.

"And now let me have a look at this passport of yours, *Father*. A real look this time. Our young friend out there is a very good shot with a rifle—claims to be able to hit a running target at three hundred yards—but the examination of documents is not his strongest point, I'm afraid. Thank you very much indeed." The man switched on a lamp over his desk and laid a magnifying glass over the passport.

"Yes, 'We, Selwyn Lloyd, request and require—' so far so good." His fat cheeks crinkled up towards his hard eyes as he studied the paper.

"But only so far, I'm afraid. The next page would pass a routine inspection, but it isn't really up to standard." He shook his head sadly and, though he spoke in German, Danilenko could recognize the Moscow accent behind it.

"But please don't take my word for it. Have a look for yourself. Whoever produced this was either hurried or rather negligent. See how the stamp over the photograph overlaps slightly and the *F* in *Foreign Office* on the paper doesn't quite join up with the rest of the word. And here, too! Why, they didn't even make sure that the ink faded evenly. Yes, even my young friend Karl Hubinger should have spotted that one." Once again came that slow, sad shake of the head—the gesture of a craftsman inspecting a botched piece of work and despising it.

"No, I'm afraid you'll have to show me something much better than this piece of incompetence, Father Parmen. You still want me to call you by that name, I take it."

"I don't mind what you call me." As Danilenko stared at him through the gloom of the hut, fear was all around him as heavy as the overcast sky outside. Away to the south a long peal of thunder rumbled across the city. Then, like a backcloth parting, the man's face smiled again and this time there was no mockery in it. It was a friendly, welcoming smile and it told him that Rima Elvoutzig hadn't failed. He was home—home and dry—and this was the contact he had come to meet.

"But I have something better to show you—much better." Danilenko smiled back and laid his right hand on the desk palm down. It was a great, gnarled hand which might have belonged to a labourer, except that the nails were long and polished. All except one, that was. The nail of the index finger was torn and bitten and looked like a ragged claw. "And may I know your name please?"

"My name?" The man grinned at the torn nail and nodded his head. "It is not important, but for the moment I answer to Schmidt as well as any other.

"Yes, that is a better passport—much better. Just what I was hoping you would show me. And there is something else which you were to carry as an introduction, I think. Thank you once again." He took the watch Danilenko held out to him and laid it beside the passport. "Yes, very, very nice. Waterproof case, self-winding mechanism, twenty-five rubies. A very expensive toy for one who has vowed to live in poverty, though I see it is five minutes slow, just as Comrade Elvoutzig said it would be.

"And now, I'm afraid the masquerade must go on a little longer, Father Parmen—or should I say, Colonel Danilenko." He got up from his desk and went to the doorway.

"Comrade Lieutenant," he said. "I am not entirely satisfied with this man's credentials. Will you be good enough to call a car and have him taken to headquarters for further questioning.

"Yes, after ten years, you should have a great many questions to answer, I think." He looked at Danilenko again and there was no smile or twinkle in his hard little eyes.

The room had a table, three steel chairs clamped to the floor, and a settee which was covered with rubber instead of fabric. It was lit by a single electric light bulb high up in the ceiling and decorated with a framed photograph of Nikita Khrushchev shaking hands with the Mayor of Berlin. There were no windows and the door looked as though it would be soundproof. Danilenko had no illusions about the sounds it was intended to conceal.

He paced backward and forward across the concrete floor, fighting to keep fear out of his mind, for there was no need for it. Schmidt had revealed himself with the statement that the masquerade must go on, and it was just a question of waiting.

Or had he revealed himself? Was Schmidt, perhaps, exactly what he seemed to be, an M.V.D. agent, and was there a traitor in the organization who had put him into his hands? No, of course he wasn't. There was no traitor, and Schmidt was certainly his contact, the man who was to give him the details of how they planned to kill Michael Kapitza. All the same, Schmidt, or whatever his real name was, might be a fool who had played it too smart by bringing him here. If he was—

Danilenko winced at the thought of either possibility.

He had no idea how long he had been in the room, though it seemed like hours. All he did know was that he was in the headquarters of one of the most ruthless organizations in the world and he had no doubts as to what would happen to him if the "Vopo" found out who he really was. On and on, yard by yard, minute by minute, he paced the grey floor and then at last looked round with a jerk as the door opened.

"Good afternoon, Colonel." The man who called himself Schmidt closed the door carefully and minced towards Danilenko with his sack-like stomach swinging before him: a little fat porker balancing on its trotters to amuse children.

"I'm very sorry to have kept you here so long, but it was necessary for the sake of appearances. Our colleagues in the People's Police always let their suspects stew for a time before a first interrogation. Let me see, just how long is it?" He consulted his watch. "Yes, over three hours, I'm afraid, but now we are quite alone and can skip the pretences. By the way, my name is Durkin—Gregor Durkin. I hope you have heard of me, Colonel."

"Yes, of course I've heard of you." His face glowing with relief, Danilenko took the pudgy hand that was held out to him. "I've heard a great deal about you—all of it good." He pumped the man's arm up and down. "But you've given me a bad time, you know. Just why did you bring me here of all places?"

"Because it seemed the best place for us to have a really private chat." Durkin glanced round the bare room. "What could be better than this little soundproof box?"

"Yes, but I still think you were taking a great risk." Relief was turning to vexation as Danilenko remembered his thoughts during those long hours, and his voice was a growl of annoyance.

"On the contrary, I risked nothing." Durkin lowered himself onto a chair and grinned. "I hold the position of M.V.D. officer attached to the Berlin police, and I have said that I am not quite satisfied with your credentials. What could be more natural than that I should bring you here and question you in comfort? Then, when we have had our talk, I shall say I was mistaken, apologize most humbly, and send you on your way rejoicing. Surely you agree with me?"

"Yes, I suppose so, but I still think you could have let me know the position at the checkpoint."

"Yes, perhaps I should have done, but all's well that ends well, Colonel. And now shall we get down to business?" Durkin leaned forward and handed him a sheet of paper.

"These are the answers to your questions. Will you memorize them, please, and then I shall destroy the paper."

"So, that's it." As Danilenko looked at the lines of typing, the paper seemed to twist and blur under his eyes, and he remembered how Kirk had dismissed his warning, and how Tania Vitgeft's body had looked in the trunk which had killed her.

"So that's how they intend to do it! Kapitza is to die as soon as he arrives in London."

"Before he actually arrives, Colonel, as you will see if you read on. He will be killed just before the launch reaches Westminster Steps."

"I see." Danilenko craned forward over the paper, studying the text, and he really did see. In his mind's eye he saw the grey river with the launch gliding in under the last of the bridges and turning towards the steps where the reception committee would be waiting to welcome their distinguished visitor. Kapitza would have to be on deck then with his hand raised in greeting probably, and a wide smile on his bearded little face. Then, just as the launch reached the steps, that smile would fade and Michael Kapitza would go down. There was no element of chance about it either. The plan required no long-range shot from a distant building. The person who killed Kapitza couldn't miss, for he would be standing at his side.

"Yes, very clever," he said. "And he has no suspicion that this has been arranged?"

"Not as far as we know, Colonel. To the best of our knowledge Kapitza thinks that all his would-be killers were eliminated last year. Besides, he has great faith in his bodyguard." Durkin smiled and his grey chins joggled up under his collar. "It's funny that, isn't it? He has great faith in his bodyguard, but one of those guards is to be his executioner."

"Yes, I suppose you could call it funny—one of his own bodyguards!" Danilenko frowned. "But there's not even a description of him—not even a name to go on. You can give me no more information than this?"

"No, that's all we can tell you, Colonel, though there's a note about our man at the foot of the page. It seems that he was once a guard or inmate at Koshuba Camp in the Urals, and that's where you come in. Isn't there a possibility that one of our members in England might once have been at Koshuba and could still recognize him?"

"Yes, I suppose it's a possibility, though a very slight one. At least it gives me something to go on, however." Danilenko's frown deepened. "But there's one thing I can't understand. This killer, whoever he is, must know that he has no chance of escape. They'll disarm him the moment Kapitza falls."

"Oh, he knows that, but perhaps it doesn't bother him. Perhaps he has been told that he will be taken back to Russia and, when all the fuss has died down, released under another name and with a handsome pension. But would you like a cigarette, Colonel?" Durkin pulled a crumpled packet and a lighter from his pocket. The lighter was heavy brass and there was a little silver star fixed to one side of it.

"Good." He watched Danilenko take a cigarette and reached out to light it for him, smiling as he did so.

"But you still don't see it, do you? You wonder how they can be so stupid. You know that, before he is allowed to be taken back to Russia, the British will insist on questioning this man, and given the right pressures, he will tell everything. And, when he talks, every radio station in the West will give full details of the plot to kill Kapitza and the people responsible will be finished.

"But the point is that the man won't talk, Colonel. He won't be allowed to talk. Look at this and I think you'll understand." Durkin handed him the lighter.

"Yes, it's clever, isn't it? On the surface a large and rather clumsy cigarette lighter, but it can become something else with a little manipulation. That's right, you've got it." He nodded again as Danilenko pressed the star on the side. As he did so a panel slid back in the base to show a tiny shining muzzle.

"Quite clever." Danilenko had seen these things before. With that adjustment the lighter became a gun firing a single cyanide pellet, and it didn't need to have much power behind it. A mere scratch from that poisoned bullet would cause instant death.

"This is what they intend to use?"

"Yes, that will be their weapon, but it's very inefficient, I'm afraid. Quite likely to explode in the user's hand, in fact." Durkin beamed on the brass cylinder as though it were his own invention.

"And supposing—just supposing—that it contained, not one, but two doses of cyanide, one for the victim and the other for his killer, then I don't think there would be any worry about anybody talking to the British. Do you understand, Colonel?"

"Yes, I understand." With a sudden wave of revulsion Danilenko handed the lighter back to him.

"Good. And now do you still think you will be able to save Kapitza?" The little man flicked the star back to "safe" and reached out for the paper in Danilenko's hand. Then he snapped on the flame. The page of typescript curled, darkened, and glowed orange.

"Well, Colonel, after what I have told you, can you save him?"

"I don't know. I don't know at all. We'll just have to see, won't we?" Danilenko looked at the burning paper and a hundred thoughts ran through his mind.

"In any case, I've only got four days, so you'd better get me out of here at once. Yes, just four days to persuade that old fool Kirk that I'm telling the truth, and also to find someone who might have known our killer at Koshuba Camp."

CHAPTER SEVEN

"Yes, Miss Bond, we're afraid that the old gentleman's fire has caused us a deal of trouble." Mr. Daniel Triggs, electrician in charge of the Ministry buildings, used the royal *we* in reference to himself. Though a very small man, he carried an air of immense importance and wore his overalls like a surgeon's gown. The array of tools spread out in front of him looked surgical, too—gleaming pliers, spanners, and screwdrivers which seemed more fitted to probing into a human body than anything so commonplace as tightening nuts and wires.

"But you did manage to fix it, I hope, Mr. Triggs." Florrie frowned as she looked at Kirk's enormous fire. "The General is going to be very put out if it isn't working."

"Oh yes, we fixed it all right, miss. There was no difficulty about that. The trouble you reported yesterday was merely a loose connection on the second switch."

"Then what's worrying you?" Florrie glanced at her watch. The time was nine fifteen and in exactly a quarter of an hour Kirk would walk into the office. He would be furious to find this pompous gnome in residence.

"It's the capacity of it, miss. The size of the thing and the amount of current it uses—to put it into nontechnical terms for a pretty young lady such as yourself. Why, in forty years of electrical engineering, we don't think we've ever seen such a powerful apparatus for heating one room. We've been wondering where the old party got hold of such a contraption."

"I believe he had it specially made for him." There was a certain bitterness in Florrie's voice as she remembered the agony of taking dictation before the horrible machine.

"Yes, quite so, miss, that's what we rather thought." Triggs shook his head solemnly, as though his worst fears had been justified. "Made by some ignorant amateur with no respect for the comfort or safety of others. You know, if the legislation of this country were in our hands, we'd have such persons under lock and key along with the quack doctors and bogus lawyers."

"I'm quite sure you would, Mr. Triggs." Florrie felt a sudden twinge of guilt for even thinking criticism of her superior. "All the same, I think General Kirk's heating arrangements are his own concern. He feels the cold very badly."

"So we have heard, Miss Bond, and of course they are his own affair. But only when they don't interfere with the comfort of others." Triggs paused and raised his hand in emphasis like a confessor driving home a point to a recalcitrant penitent.

"As we were saying to our wife only yesterday—she's somewhat younger than ourself and inclined to be headstrong—'Betty,' we said, 'by all means hang your washing out in the garden, but not during the weekends when our neighbours are at home and wish to enjoy the view; not when it interferes with the pleasure and comfort of others.'"

"But what on earth has that got to do with the General's fire?" Great waves of sympathy for "our" wife flowed through Florrie's head.

"It's because of the fuses, miss—the power fuses for this floor—they just won't take the load. Why, he's got four bars of fifteen hundred watts each on this contraption—six kilowatts!" He shook his head again and started to gather up his tools, wiping each one carefully before tucking it into a leather bag.

"Then couldn't you put in bigger fuses?"

"What's that you say, miss?" A screwdriver clattered from his hand and he gaped at her in astonishment. "Put in bigger fuses and risk damaging the wiring! Why, that would be against all our professional code. What would the resident engineer say if he heard of such a thing? What would the Minister himself say? 'Mr. Triggs has put in bigger fuses and risked damaging the wiring!' They just wouldn't believe it possible, Miss Bond, and we're surprised you should even consider such an idea." He picked up the screwdriver and squinted at the blade as though fearing it might be damaged.

"All the same, we have done something to deal with this problem. We won't bore you with the technical details, but just look at this little box we've screwed on here. That's the warning system."

"The warning system?"

"Yes, an alarm which will tell you when it's safe to run the machine at full power." He bent down and pressed the first switch. Almost at once the two lower bars broke into a cheery glow.

"Now that's always in order. It's also quite all right to use the other two bars providing the rest of the floor is not consuming a great deal of current. But suppose—just suppose—that a lot of other people were using power." He shook a gnarled finger at her. "Mrs. Hamble in the decoding room might like a nice warm fire now and then—Mr. Virgo in Files—that Russian gentleman with the odd name in the next corridor. If that were the case, as soon as the old gentlemen turned this contraption on full, all the fuses would blow and then where would you be?"

"In the dark, I suppose, but I gather that's not to happen?"

"No, this warning system will see to that, miss. A very clever arrangement, though we say so ourselves, and we'll show you how it works. Our assistant has turned on all the fires in the other rooms to give you an example. Now, just you listen."

Triggs paused for a moment like a conjurer preparing for the final trick which would hold his audience spellbound, and then pressed the second switch. As he did so, Florrie almost jumped in astonishment. For from the box there came a scream as of human agony—the howl of a soul in the last stages of some nameless torment. Triggs smiled smugly and switched it off again.

"There you are, miss, and very efficient it is, as we think

you'll agree. As soon as you hear that warning you'll know that it's time to turn off the upper bars, or all the fuses will blow."

"We most certainly will." She stared at him in horror. "But the General's not going to like it one little bit."

"Perhaps he won't at the beginning, but he'll soon get accustomed to it. Yes, we're afraid the old gentleman will just have to control his passion for heat. Of course, it will be quite all right during the summer months when other people are not using their fires, and that will give him time to get accustomed to the idea.

"And now we must be getting on our way, Miss Bond. The janitor tells us that one of the lift buttons is sticking rather badly, and it would never do for us to let anybody get stranded between floors, would it?" Triggs closed his tool bag with a snap, gave Florrie a fine courtly bow, and strutted off out of the room.

"Morning, my dear. What did that little pomposity want?" Kirk had obviously passed Triggs in the outer office. "Oh, fixed the fire, has he? High time, too. Now we can have a bit of comfort at last." To her consternation he bent down and switched on the upper bars. They glowed brightly, but this time no sound came from the warning device. Mercifully "our" assistant must have turned off the fires in the other rooms.

"Yes, that's better. Now I can feel it." Kirk beamed with satisfaction and settled himself down behind his desk. "Any messages since I left last night?"

"A couple of telephone calls, sir. Colonel Danilenko rang a few minutes ago. He said it was most urgent that he see you as soon as possible."

"Oh no, not that blasted fellow again." Kirk groaned loudly. "Urgent indeed! Of course he said it was urgent. Everything the man said or does is urgent—to himself. Did he tell you what it was about?"

"Yes, sir." Florrie consulted her diary. "He said that he had got definite confirmation that he was right about the M.K. affair."

"The devil he did!" Kirk leaned far back in his chair. No, it was impossible, he thought, quite impossible. His talk with Martin Wilde had cleared that matter up. All the same—

"Yes, I suppose I'd better see him. Ring the fellow up and tell him to meet me at my club, will you? No, not for lunch. Half an hour and a cup of coffee at eleven is the only time and entertainment I intend to waste on Colonel Bogus. . . . And the second call?"

"It was from the Belworth police, sir. They want to know if it is all right for them to hand over the Vitgeft house to the auctioneers again."

"Um, I don't see why not. They and the Special Branch have been over the place with a fine-tooth comb and they won't find anything else. Have the keys sent over to them."

"Yes sir, but I was wondering if—" Florrie broke off before completing the sentence. She had only worked with Kirk since Miss Colman had been called away to nurse her aged relative, and she wasn't sure how he would react to a personal request.

"You were wondering what?" Kirk had already started to go through his mail and he didn't look up at her.

"It's about Princess Vitgeft's house, sir. When I typed out our copies of the inventory, I noticed that there were a lot of books."

"Yes, I believe there were, but what about it?"

"Well, I wanted to ask if I could have a look at them, sir. You see a friend of mine runs a second-hand bookshop near Belworth, and if the books are any good, he might like to buy them."

"My dear Miss Bond, what are you talking about? Just what has your friend's shop to do with me?" Kirk frowned up at her. He had been pleased when he came into the office and found his fire working, but pleasure was rapidly turning to irritation.

"It's just that I want to help him so much, sir. You see he hasn't been very long in business and is desperate for stock. If I could list the Vitgeft books for him, he might be able to make the auctioneer a private offer before they came up for sale."

"I see." Kirk considered for a moment and then nodded. "Rather a sharp way of doing business, perhaps, but I can't see too much harm in it. Type yourself out a pass and I'll sign it before I go.

"And now, I think that we both have work to do." He bent over his letters again feeling rather sorry for himself. Florrie might be a very pretty girl and an ornament to any office, but he decided that he really would be pleased to see the grim-faced Miss Colman back in harness.

"So you see, General, we have to do something now." Danilenko stared across the big gloomy room of plush and mahogany, thinking that Kirk's club was a pleasant but very decadent place. All around them old gentlemen dozed in deep armchairs, waiters moved softly across the thick, though faded, carpet, and apart from their voices and a slight rustle of newspapers, the silence was unbroken. He decided that it was part of a world which was dying anyway, but might go on a little longer if Michael Kapitza were to live.

"We know quite definitely what they have planned now—where and how he is to die, and we must take action to stop it."

"*We* know!" Kirk raised his eyebrows slightly. "But *I* don't know. To the best of my belief the assassination was planned over a year ago and frustrated in Russia. I don't want to be rude, Colonel, but all I have to go on is what you have just told me."

"Yes, what I have told you, General. What I went into East Germany to find out for you." To the fury of an old gentleman who had been peacefully sleeping in a chair on their right, the Russian's hand crashed down on the table. There was no anger in Danilenko's face, though—only a plea. The expression of a child begging to be believed that he really has seen Santa Claus.

"But what did you expect from me? To walk back across the border with a copy of his death warrant in my pocket? To show you a letter signed by the people who have arranged to

kill him? General Kirk, I risked my life to get you that information. My comrade, Gregor Durkin, risks his every minute
he sits in that M.V.D. office. He also told me that at least three
people had died to find out those details. You must believe that
I am telling you the truth. For the sake of ourselves and the
free world you must. Unless you do, Kapitza will be shot down
the moment his launch reaches Westminster Steps."

"You say that I *must* believe you." Kirk's frown deepened
and he recalled the words of the first Elizabeth: "Little man,
must is not a word to use with princes." He was no prince and
Danilenko was a giant, but the man's arrogance infuriated
him.

"But even if I do believe you, Colonel, what action do you
expect me to take? Do you think I can walk into the Soviet
Embassy and tell them that the L.W.R., an organization with
the avowed aim of destroying their political system, has
informed me that Kapitza is to be murdered by one of his own
bodyguard, a man with no name, no photograph, not even a
description? And supposing that I went to my superiors and
said that because of what you have told me I refuse to guarantee his safety, what do you think would happen? I'm quite sure
there would be somebody else sitting behind my desk before
the week was out."

"Courage, my friend! We haven't lost yet—not by a long
chalk, as you say." Danilenko's face broke into a smile and,
to Kirk's disgust, he reached out and squeezed his arm. Kirk
pulled it hurriedly away, but not before the old gentleman on
their right had noted the action and glowered at them. The
world was in a poor way, he seemed to be thinking. The stock
market down again, the last Australian collapse had made
mockery of first-class cricket, and now this club was getting
some very queer fish on its membership.

"No, not by a long chalk are we finished, General. As long as
you trust me we can forestall this assassination." Quite oblivious of the effect he was creating, Danilenko beamed at him.

"You see, we still have one card up our sleeve and it may be the ace of trumps. Apart from the fact that Kapitza's killer is a member of his bodyguard, we know that between 1945 and '47 he was a guard or inmate at Koshuba Concentration Camp."

"And so?" Kirk pulled at his cigar and studied the Russian's face through the drifting smoke. If Danilenko's story were true, it was his clear duty to act on it. On the other hand, he still didn't completely trust him, and for all he knew, the story might have been invented to make the L.W.R. seem important.

"And so that is the card we must play, General. Koshuba Camp and the face of a man who was once a guard or an inmate there. As you know, Koshuba was a small prison, but not a pleasant one. It was reserved for people with doubts. Useful people who were sent there to be cured of their doubts and returned to work for the good of the state: doctors, teachers, engineers, people of value. The means used to cure them were said to be very thorough and I don't think that any prisoner at Koshuba would be likely to forget a face she had known there."

"She! You mean you've found one of them?" Kirk sat bolt upright staring at him, and he knew exactly what he would have to do if Danilenko were telling the truth. He imagined the Russian bodyguard grouped around Kapitza—one of them his executioner, a faceless, nameless man in a tight suit, standing in the launch and watching the London skyline creep closer. A man who thought he would be rewarded for what he did, reaching in his pocket for a little trick gun that contained two poisoned bullets. And, just before he used it, and sent the hopes of the world crashing down, a woman who had once been a prisoner at Koshuba would nod her head towards one of Kirk's men and the matter would be finished.

"Oh yes, I've found one of them for you, General. I've done rather better than that, in fact. I've been to see her and discussed our terms." If possible, the Russian's grin seemed to grow even wider, hinging his face into a great black cavern to show a line of gold teeth like a treasure trove.

"But tell me something," he said. "How much would you say that Kapitza is worth in terms of money? How many billion pounds and dollars will be wiped from the stock markets if he dies? By how many millions will armament shares fall if he lives and succeeds Khrushchev? No, don't try to guess, I'll tell you exactly how much he is worth." He raised his hand like a schoolmaster quelling an overeager class.

"As I said, I've talked to this lady and come to terms. Assuming that she is able to recognize our killer, all we need to guarantee the safety of Michael Kapitza is a cash payment of three thousand pounds."

But though Danilenko claimed that he knew how to save Kapitza, there were other people who were just as certain that they could kill him.

They sat in a house off the Nevski Prospekt in Leningrad, and though one of them was a woman and their faces bore at least four different racial characteristics, their expressions were the same—expressions which might have been cast in a single mould—and they showed authority and ruthlessness and arrogance that only years of power can produce. The faces of the Old Guard, the old unrelenting Bolsheviks who would never change till death or disease withered them.

"Well, Marshal, we are waiting for you, it seems." The woman sat at the head of the table smiling down along the row of faces. Her Russian was technically faultless, but the accent marked her as a foreigner. "You are the only one of us who has not yet voted."

"Very well, Comrade, I agree." Very slowly the soldier raised his hand, but he didn't look at the woman. He hated even being in the same room with her. Her name was Paula Stein—sometime Communist delegate for the Wedding district of Berlin—sometime inmate of Ravensbruck Concentration Camp—at the moment the owner of a little plastic card which stated that she was second in command of all Soviet Intelligence Services in Europe.

"Yes, I agree. Michael Kapitza must die." The soldier felt

that he might be signing his own death warrant as he said it. "We know that should he ever succeed Khrushchev every one of us here would be finished. I also believe that very soon afterwards the Party itself would be finished. So he must die. But I am still worried about the manner of his death."

"I understand, Marshal. I understand all of you." Paula Stein stood up and stopped smiling. Her waist barely reached the top of the table, but she seemed to dominate the room like a lion-tamer in a cage of heavily drugged animals.

"Yes, I understand you—Russians. You want to kill Kapitza because he threatens your power, but you are frightened. You know that if anything goes wrong—if there is the slightest suspicion that you planned his death—you will be put against a wall and shot. Always provided that a lynching mob doesn't find you first. But give me a match please, Konstantin Zinovitch." She took a cigarette from a box at her side, and very humbly an admiral of the fleet stood up and lit it for her.

"Russians," she said. "Old, tired Russians—little frightened Russians. Part of a nation that is just down from the trees, and could have done nothing without the help of the German technicians you took after the war." She dragged hard at the cigarette and stared at them through the smoke.

"Well, children, I am one of those technicians, and there is nothing to worry about, because I have planned things well for you. You will face no firing squad, and no mob will come to tear you to pieces. You can sleep quite peacefully in your beds, meine Herren." There was no mistaking the contempt in her voice as she used the German words.

"Yes, Comrade Marshal, Comrade Minister, Comrade Professor, all of you. There will be no mistake this time and everything has been arranged to the last detail. Kapitza will die exactly two minutes before he steps ashore in London, and an hour later the whole world will know that he was murdered by the British Intelligence Service on orders from their American masters."

CHAPTER EIGHT

Mrs. Sophia Robinson liked being alone and she liked watching the vapour trails. She leaned against the gate of the farm, looking eastward, and from where she stood they were like lattice-work across the sky. Little silver and gold threads that soon thickened in the wind to become drifting tapeworms of cloud. And, always in front of them, was the tiny dot of a B.64 bomber.

Yes, that little dot was always there. One up in the sky and one on the airstrip ready and waiting to take its place. Twenty-four hours a day, seven days a week, fifty-two weeks a year. Tiny glittering wedges with the great deterrent in their bellies circling over the flat East Anglian landscape: wide fields, and parallel ditches, and the tall churches that stood out like ships on every horizon.

She turned slightly towards the wind, feeling it fresh and clean on her face, and hearing the sound of Mike's tractor in the far distance. Even from half a mile away it sounded harsh and uneven. If the motor wasn't renewed before long, there would be no ploughing that autumn. Like everything else on the farm it was worn out and defeated.

And it had all been so different once; promise and hope and a future. She remembered the long convoys drawn up against the dock at Solombola, and the boys jumping off the lurching trams before the Archangel Club. British and American uniforms mingling with the light brown of the Red Army, and a three-piece band playing "Russian Rose." And Mike dancing with her, and admiring the new dress which the Intourist organization had given her to entertain their allies. Mike laughing too sometimes, but not very loudly, because they'd had a bad time coming round the North Cape that convoy.

Mike smiling at her across the smoke and the vodka fumes in the dance hall, and walking her home along the crumbling wooden pavements, past the ever-present statues of Lenin. Mike holding her tight in the bed which was made up on top of a stove and telling her that he would come and fetch her when the war was over, while, in the square outside, the People's Radio blared out martial music and the news of victories.

But soon it had finished. The cargoes were unloaded, the holds were filled with timber before ice gripped the river, and the ships left. Squat, ugly ships with names that all started in the same way; *Samammon*, *Samsulva*, *Samgara*, *Samlyth*, sailing away between the green banks of the Dvina with the children waving and shouting "Goodbye, Johnnie" from the anchored barges.

And afterwards? No, she didn't want to think of the immediate afterwards. How they had taken her away when Mike's first letter arrived and the long train journey to the place where hope died. Rooms where the furniture was clamped to the floor, faces that always looked the same, and voices that always said the same thing—"If you marry this Englishman there will be a debt to pay. If you marry him—if you marry—a debt—a debt—a debt—"

No, she didn't want to think about that, or how she had finally got out. Only the present mattered now. The last year's crop which had failed, the mortgage which was long overdue, and the letters that came too regularly. "My dear daughter, please remember your promise. . . . Darling Sophie, you must try to help us." Such a lot of letters and they all carried the same message—"Remember." She pushed it out of her mind and thought about herself. Mrs. Sophia Petrovna Robinson, aged thirty-seven but looking fifty, with a husband and two children whom she loved, but who could probably get on very well without her. Mrs. Robinson who felt she had died a long time ago.

Not that the feeling bothered her greatly as she considered life. Bodies twisting and mingling together to produce it.

Lying and breeding together—dying together. Millions of them under the soil of this one country alone, she imagined. Manuring and feeding the earth to bring round fruitfulness again. Conception, gestation, rebirth, generation. Families of plants and animals springing up from the cold bodies of the dead. The thought sickened her.

But now everything was coming to an end. She had made her decision and would do what she had been asked to do. The only reward she wanted was that Mike's mortgage would be paid off. She turned from the gate and fixed her face into an automatic smile as the pennant-bearing car swung into the yard and two men climbed heavily out.

The first man she knew, of course. A huge man whose body looked as though it had been roughly carved out of teak, and whose walk was a march. She hated the type he represented. The professional soldier who has worn uniform most of his life and feels ill at ease out of it.

But it was the second man who interested her. Though he was a soldier too, he looked quite different, almost ineffectual in fact, with his thick coat wrapped tightly around him, as though it were January instead of midsummer, hat pulled low down over his forehead and a grey moustache almost touching his muffler. Then, as she took his hand, she knew that there was nothing ineffectual about him. His eyes seemed to look right through her and see the loneliness and fear under her worn face. She felt like a naked child beneath the stare of Kirk's mild eyes.

"Well, Mrs. Robinson, we have come to give you the final briefing." Danilenko followed her into the little gloomy kitchen of the farmhouse. "We are quite alone here, I hope."

"Yes, we're alone, Colonel. My husband is out at work, and my children are at school." She leaned back against the table and struggled for what she had to say—what Kirk's stare told her she must say.

"But I'm not sure, gentlemen. I've been thinking it over, and I'm not sure if I can do what you ask."

"Not sure, Mrs. Robinson!" Danilenko lowered his bulk onto a chair and flashed a great lazy smile at her. "But it was all decided. I went to a lot of trouble to find you, and you are probably the only survivor of Koshuba Camp in this country—the only person who can help us, in fact. Now I have brought my friend, General Kirk, to see you and you can't let him down. A full general! A very important man indeed!"

"I don't want to let anybody down. It's just that—" She broke off, turning away from the Russian and looking at Kirk. "General, I do want to help, but please try and understand. You see, I have a family in Russia."

"Yes, I know that, Mrs. Robinson." Kirk nodded his head slightly. "You have a mother in Kiev and two sisters in Moscow. Would you mind if I smoked?

"Thank you." He lit a cigar and studied the woman's face as he did so, seeing the bleakness of it and the loneliness in it, and remembered what Danilenko had told him about her past. A love-affair with a British sailor that had led to a concentration camp. Two and a half years there, followed by contemptuous dismissal and the promise that there were always hostages for her good behaviour.

"And it is just because of your family that we are asking you to help us—for the sake of everybody's family. Certain people in Russia are hoping to kill Michael Kapitza and, if they succeed, the camps like Koshuba will go on. The barbed wire will continue to stretch across Europe. Your family will continue to live in fear. Do you want that, Mrs. Robinson? If you do, please tell me so and we will walk out of your house now."

"No, I don't want it, General, but please try to understand. Can't you see that—" With a quick compulsive movement she turned away from them and pulled open the back of her blouse. The flesh under it was a mass of white scars, and Kirk knew at once what had made them. The Russian knout was the only instrument of torture that cut with those exact parallel lines.

"Yes, it's pleasant, isn't it, gentlemen?" she said. "And do you think I can risk that happening to my mother? Can you ask me to risk that?"

"We are not asking you to do anything, Sophie Petrovna, we are ordering you." Danilenko got up from his chair and stood towering over her like a mountain. He still wore that great lazy smile, but his neck muscles were straining against his collar. He raised his hand and, for a moment, Kirk thought he was about to strike the woman, but all he did was to pull back the blouse over her shoulder.

"Yes, Sophie," he said. "You are going to do exactly what we say, and there is no need to worry about the Soviet police or the M.V.D.; most of them are as eager to protect Kapitza as we are." He tilted her face up to his, and Kirk could see that she was weeping.

"No, there is nothing at all to be worried about. You will be given another name and wear an interpreter's uniform. You will have a disguise, too: a wig perhaps, and rubber pads to fill out your poor thin cheeks. Nobody will know who you are, and all you have to do is to stand in a boat and try to remember a face you knew at Koshuba. Surely you will do that for us?"

"Yes, I'll do it." The woman had looked small when they had first seen her, but now she seemed tiny—a little shrivelled doll, broken and thrown away by children. "I don't think I could forget any face I knew at Koshuba."

"Good." Kirk crossed towards them. He felt horribly embarrassed, like someone who has walked into a very private quarrel between husband and wife.

"I am most grateful that you have decided to help us, Mrs. Robinson, and we will make it as easy as we can for you. As you know, Kapitza is due to arrive at six o'clock on Monday evening. At midday one of my men will pick you up here and take you to Southend where Kapitza transfers from the Russian cruiser. All you have to do is to stand on the launch and try to point out anybody you remember seeing at that camp. You'll do that for me, won't you, my dear?" When he saw her slow, tired nod, he smiled.

"Thank you. I was sure we could rely on you. And now we'll leave you in peace. Are you coming, Colonel?"

"In a moment, General Kirk, in just one moment." Danilenko watched him move out of the room, and then he lifted his hand and tilted the woman's face up to his again.

"Yes, little Sophie," he said, and only the cliché of iron beneath the velvet could describe his voice. "You will do exactly what we tell you to do, and there is nothing to be frightened of. Nothing to fear from the Soviet police, or the M.V.D., or anything in the world. Nothing—except me." He moved away from her to the door, and then turned and looked back with his hand resting on the knob.

"You understand me, don't you, Sophie Petrovna?"

"Yes, I understand you, Colonel, there is nothing to fear except you." The woman stood quite still, staring at the floor as he moved away. Then, as the car started, she walked across to the window and threw it open.

It was evening now. Very soon Mike and the children would be coming in for their tea, but she still had a little time left for her own thoughts. She turned her face to the wind and breathed the cool air. Far away towards the east there was a dark ridge of cloud drifting in from the sea and threatening rain. And, also from the east, something else was coming. The Soviet cruiser, *Dimitri Donskoi*, which carried a man who had been condemned to death.

She pushed the thought from her mind and stared out across the flat landscape which gave her peace. Wide fields and parallel ditches, and tall churches standing out like ships on every horizon. And always above it, twenty-four hours a day, seven days a week, fifty-two weeks a year, the vapour trails of the American bombers which told her that hatred and fear were still alive—vapour trails widening.

CHAPTER NINE

By six o'clock Florrie Bond decided she had had one hell of a day and was beginning to hate the very name Kapitza. Almost from the moment that Kirk left the office to meet Danilenko the phone had started to ring, and it had gone on ringing without a break. Most of the calls were purely formal, of course, relayed to them by Scotland Yard, but they still had to be answered and transcribed. Calls from the Admiralty giving the details of where the Soviet cruiser would anchor, and the exact procedure of Kapitza's transfer to the launch. A call from the Claymore Hotel with a query about the seating arrangements for the dinner party to be given in his honour on the second day. A long involved message from traffic control concerning the route he would take from Richmond Park on the formal drive to Buckingham Palace. Even a call from the Oval cricket ground where he was to attend the opening day of a match between Surrey and Australia.

"Ring—ring—ring!" After three hours of it her hand was like an automatic lever lifting the phone and her voice sounded just as automatic. "Yes, Superintendent, I'll see that General Kirk has your message first thing in the morning. The procession will leave the White Lodge at eleven and proceed along the Upper Richmond Road and Chiswick Bridge, passing Hammersmith at eleven twenty. They will then go via the Cromwell Road extension and Knightsbridge to reach the palace at a quarter to twelve. Yes, we know about your rehearsals, and an escort of twelve motorcycles will be quite satisfactory." The phone going down, the whir of a tape recorder, and then another ring. "Good afternoon, Admiral. Yes, that is correct. There will be twenty-three people in the Russian party, and we want ten of our own personnel in the launch. That's right, six of them will be in naval uniform and the rest in civilian clothes. No, I'm very sorry, but I don't think we could possibly cut down on those numbers. Perhaps you'd like the General to ring you when he gets back to the office."

Phew! She felt limp and ill-tempered when at last she handed over the phone to her opposite number on the night staff. Six o'clock and she hadn't even had a proper break for lunch. Saturday evening, too, for Kirk's office never closed at the week-ends. When Miss Colman had departed to her parent's sickbed, Florrie had felt great excitement at taking on her job, but that was all finished now, and thoughts of other easier forms of earning a living flicked through her head. A nice comfortable position in the Ministry of Health, for example. Long chats about clothes and hair styles, and innumerable cups of tea over the medical cards. Better still if her boy-friend's business would start to expand and she could go and work for him. Yes, she'd be very happy there.

"Cheer up, Flo." Mrs. Annie Baxter, her relief, was stout and middle-aged and had given up clock-watching years ago. "You'll be off on Monday, won't you, dear?"

"No, not a chance of it. I'm due to be off, but with this Kapitza business everything's gone haywire. What have you got there, Annie?"

"They were on the desk, dear." Mrs. Baxter jangled a bunch of keys in her plump little hand. "Thought they were yours."

"Oh yes, of course." Florrie finished repairing her face and took them from her. "They're the keys of that Vitgeft house—you know, the woman who was murdered last year. The General asked me to return them to the police, as there's nothing more to be found there. With that phone going all day, I completely forgot about them. Thanks for reminding me." She slipped them into her handbag beside the pass that Kirk had signed for her.

"I'll go over there now, I think. The house is only a mile or two from Tom's shop, and I'm not meeting him till eight."

"Tom? Oh yes, Tom Valley, the bookseller." Mrs. Baxter

interested herself keenly in the love-affairs of others. "How is he getting on since he started on his own?"

"Pretty well, I think, but the trouble is that he never seems to be able to find enough books. I don't really understand the second-hand trade, but apparently it's always more difficult to get hold of good stock than to sell it. That's why I'm going round to the Vitgeft house now. It seems that the contents are going to be handed back to the auctioneers and I'm going to have a preview. General Kirk gave me a pass to get in."

"Well, good hunting, dear. I hope you find a First Folio, or whatever it is that's so valuable. 'Night, Flo." Annie Baxter grinned at her and then reached forward as the phone rang again.

" 'Night, Annie." Florrie went through into the outer office and put on her coat. As she did so, she seemed to hear Tom Valley's voice with its constant complaint about the shortage of stock. "If only I could get hold of some decent books once in a while we could start to branch out. The trouble is that all anybody thinks about these days is selling to America, and the country's been bled white."

Well, perhaps she might be able to find some stock for him. What was the number of the Vitgeft file again? Yes, Ninety-two. She pulled open the drawer of a filing cabinet and took it out. As Kirk had said, nothing of any importance had been found in the house. Nothing to throw any light on the murder or that garbled message which foretold the death of Kapitza. No papers stuffed away in a secret drawer—no tell-tale fingerprints—no transmitter hidden behind the panelling. All the file contained was the report of a completely blank search, and the inventory typed out on Hyde, Herod & Scott's tasteful notepaper: "Carpets, 7—all badly worn and stained. Tables, 8—none of any antique value. Desks, 2—both worm-infested. Books—" Yes, here she was. "Approximately 200 volumes containing an interesting collection of material on the Russo-Japanese war of 1904–5."

"Yes, I wonder." She muttered the words aloud to the accompaniment of Mrs. Baxter's voice on the telephone. "If the books are any good, I wonder if this Hyde, Herod & Scott would play ball." There wasn't anything of great value among Tania Vitgeft's possessions, and by the look of their paper they seemed to be a rich, self-important firm. If Tom had a detailed list of the books he could make them a good private offer, and they might be willing to sell without going to the trouble of a public auction. All a bit unethical, perhaps, but she wouldn't let that worry her. She replaced the file and went out.

And, as she had hoped, there was no crowd of sightseers in Benham Grove. The department and the police had made the Press play down the discovery of Vitgeft's body, and apart from two children at the top of the street, a young man bent over a motor bicycle, and a woman mowing her front lawn, it was deserted. The house itself stood rather back from its neighbours, and the unclipped bushes which had grown into fair-size trees seemed to cut it off like a little private world of its own. She pulled back the sagging gate and walked down the path, smelling a tang of rank tobacco smoke as she did so.

"Evenin'." The man came round from the side of the porch, looking completely at home. He would probably look like that anywhere, for he had been trained to loiter unobtrusively and was very good at it. A large comfortable man of a type one associated with the British Legion and saloon bars and bowling clubs. A man who could stand by the door of a bank for hours and never be noticed because he was so obviously waiting for a friend, or lean against a pub counter hearing and seeing everything without drawing the slightest attention to himself.

"Oh, it's Miss Bond, isn't it?" They had met when Florrie had been sent round to the police station to collect a typescript of the evidence and he seemed pleased to see a familiar face. "And what can I do for you, miss?"

"Hullo, officer." Florrie grinned back at him. "I didn't expect you'd still be here."

"And neither did I, miss." He leaned comfortably back against the wall and knocked out his pipe. "Can't see any sense in it, in fact. Three days now we've been hangin' around this dump, me and Pounder and Sims, and never a sign of anything suspicious. Couple of reporters came round, a young fellow from the agents, and that's the lot. Bloomin' waste of public money if you ask me. Murderers may be said to return to the scene of their crimes, but not after a year they don't. Bored stiff I am, Miss Bond, and I don't mind who knows it." There was a far-away look in his eyes, and he might have been thinking of a pint of bitter at the local, followed by steak and two veg and a pleasant evening in front of the telly.

"I'm sure you are, officer, and I'm afraid it may be my fault that you're still here. General Kirk told me this morning that we had no objection to your handing back the house to the estate agents, but I've been so tied up today that I never got round to ringing the station."

"Oh, that's all right, miss. After all, I get paid for it." He hitched his coat a little higher in preparation for departure and looked at her car parked against the pavement.

"It's very nice of you to come round and tell me—very nice indeed. Now, if you'd give me a lift back in that little motor of yours, I'd be still more obliged."

"I'm afraid I can't just at the moment." Florrie pulled Kirk's pass from her handbag. "I was told to make a quick check through the bookcases before returning the keys."

"Um, I see." Rather sadly the man studied the paper and then handed it back to her. "Well, let's get on with it, if that's what they want." He started to move towards the door with an air of dumb resignation.

"No, no, there's no need for you to hang about, officer. It'll only take me a few minutes—just a quick routine check in case anything was missed. I'll drop the keys in at the station as soon as I've finished."

"Well, if you're sure that's all right, Miss Bond. I can't say that I won't be sorry to get along home." There was a marked relief in his face. "As it happens, there's a darts match at my local that I was rather hoping to attend."

"Of course I'm sure, officer. You get along to your darts, and I'll be quite all right."

"Very well then, I'll be on my way. It won't take you long to go through a few old books, but I doubt if you'll find anything. They went through the place with a fine-tooth comb." He watched her pull out the keys, then moved in front of her to open the door with a skeleton set of his own. "Allow me, though, miss. The atmosphere's a bit unpleasant in there, but there's nothing to be frightened of."

"Of course there isn't. Now you go along, officer. I'll manage all right."

"I'm sure you will." He held open the door and beamed at her. "Good night then, Miss Bond, and all the best to you."

"Good night, officer." Florrie watched him move ponderously down the path. Then she walked through the doorway.

The house was clean now. It had been searched for fingerprints and footmarks, and vacuum-cleaners had removed the dust for analysis. All the same, there are things that no brush or cleaner can remove. The odour of dry rot fanned up through the floor, and the stale atmosphere of neglect and disrepair hung over the building like a physical gas. She crossed into the library, seeing the three tall cases of books against the wall and neat pile of them by the door, and she remembered how Tania Vitgeft had died. An old frail body thrown into a trunk while it was still alive, and left to mummify beneath the musty volumes. Kirk and the police held the theory that the murderer had been disturbed before he could remove the body, but a rather more unpleasant one came into her mind. Was the object of the killing not just death, but death by torture? Had Tania Vitgeft made such a nuisance of herself to the M.V.D. that they decided she was to pay the fullest possible penalty?

Yes, as the policeman had said, there was a very nasty atmosphere in the house. She glanced at one pile of books and walked quickly past them. Whatever she felt for Tom, she couldn't touch those. Most probably it was under those very books that old Tania's body had withered.

Still, if she was to do her job, she had better keep her mind off the murder. She pulled out a pen and notebook, and started to check the books in the first case the way Bob had shown her, listing them under *Author, Title, Date of Publication*, and coding the condition into four categories. *Fine, Very Good, Good* and *Reading Copy*. *Good* meant that a book was in a pretty poor state, and *Reading Copy* that you could just open it before the pages fell to pieces. She turned quickly as something rustled beside her feet, and saw a mouse regarding her gravely for a moment before scurrying under a gap in the wainscot.

But there was nothing much in the first bookcase. Memoirs of people who had been forgotten years ago. Novels that might once have been thought works of genius, but now were waste paper, though occasionally mentioned as memory tests. "Let me see—*The Bulls of Monserrat*? Yes, wasn't it written by a man called Redfern, back in the twenties?" Out-of-date encyclopaedias, unsaleable poetry, and the *Works of Shakespeare* in double columns of tiny print. No, Tom wouldn't thank her for listing this lot. She turned to the second case, and almost at once her eyes brightened.

Yes! ". . . containing an interesting collection of material on the Russo-Japanese War of 1904–5," Hyde, Herod & Scott's list had read, and here it was. Though she was very much an amateur, she did know that naval history was one of Tom's interests, and she took a lot of care with the list, thumbing through each volume to check—no, that wasn't the word—to *collate* the plates.

Yes—Fred T. Jane's *Imperial Russian Navy*, all correct, with illustrations of archaic ships that looked as if they couldn't even float, belching thick clouds of smoke. Priboi's *Battle of Tsushima*, no plates to be checked in that one, thank goodness. Klado's *Sea of Japan*, correct, though the spine was badly worn. And here, at the very end of the shelf, a book she had heard Tom mention, *Rasplata* or *The Reckoning* by Vladimir Semenoff. Yes, she seemed to remember that that one was worth something. Hadn't he said that he had a customer for it, too? She stared at the decorated cover with its two-headed eagle against a faded orange background and flicked the book open at the title page: "A DIARY KEPT DURING THE BLOCKADE OF PORT ARTHUR AND THE VOYAGE OF ADMIRAL ROJESTVEN-SKY'S FLEET."

No plates to check again, but the rather flamboyant style attracted her, and she browsed through the pages, fascinated by the story of folly and incompetence that they told. The doomed ships ploughing through the night, and two officers pacing a bridge and knowing that the daylight could only bring disaster: "We have come so far, and we shall go farther yet— We are going—? I don't recollect— Oh yes, of course—to our reckoning." She suddenly though, of another Russian warship as she read the words—the Soviet cruiser, *Dimitri Donskoi*, which would already be carrying Michael Kapitza through the Baltic. Would he also find that there was a reckoning to be paid at journey's end? she wondered.

She noted the date and particulars of the edition, and started to close the book. As she did so she stiffened, for there was something wrong. It wouldn't close properly and there seemed to be something wedged between the back cover and the endpapers to prevent it lying flat. Yes, there certainly was: a little pocket glued to the cardboard with a lip of grey paper showing through it. She pulled at the paper, and all thoughts of Tom Valley and the book trade vanished from her mind. Could this be something that they had missed—something which the police and the department had failed to find? A letter that might somehow show why Tania Vitgeft had died?

But no, there was nothing like that. Merely a collection of newspaper photographs to illustrate the text. Pictures of bearded officers covered with medals and gold braid; pictures of ironclads steaming towards destruction, with printed captions beneath them: "The cruiser, *Varyag*, at Chemulpo, June 29th. . . . The battleships, *Retvizan* and *Pobeba*, after the bombardment, *sic transit gloria mundi*."

But here—yes—here there was a letter! Two letters in fact!

Five pages of faded grey paper tucked in behind the last photograph. She turned the first page to the light and stared at the writing. It was in German and the date proved that it had nothing to do with the Battle of Tsushima. "London—1882." It had nothing to do with the murder of Tania Vitgeft either and had been written years before the woman was even born. She was almost on the point of pushing it back into the book when something familiar struck her about the form of address and she stiffened—"London, July 2nd 1882. *Mein Lieber* Fred . . ."

But where was it? Just where had she seen that slightly comic mixture of English and German before? She carried the letters to the window, frowning as she struggled to translate.

"Mein Lieber Fred . . ." Her German was pretty rusty and the faded writing was difficult to decipher, but very slowly she pieced the text together: "Yes, as I told you before, it would be most pleasant if Wedde's plan for a really scientific socialist journal could come about. In that way we could expose the utter ignorance of the university gentlemen and educate the minds of the general public . . ."

Yes, that style was certainly familiar. She had once taken an extra-mural course in Economics and the memory of long dull hours bent over similar letters was very close to her. There was a gleam of excitement in her eyes as she stared at the scribbled signature at the foot of the last page. If these letters turned out to be not merely printed facsimiles but originals she might bring Tom something much more valuable than a list of medium-priced books. A small fortune, in fact— the treasure trove every dealer prays to find once in a lifetime but rarely does. Once again her fingers ran lovingly across the brittle pages; then she pushed them into her handbag.

In London the time was eight o'clock and Kirk and Danilenko were driving home through the eastern suburbs. They had dined well and leaned far back against the car cushions with the air of men who had carried out a difficult piece of business to their full satisfaction and were at peace with the world.

In Berlin it was almost nine and Gregor Durkin was sitting outside his favourite café on the "Linden," enjoying a glass of cool white wine and knowing that he had done all that was expected of him.

In the Gulf of Finland it was ten and a Russian security officer named Ivan Andreyevitch Petrov smiled at the fading coastline as the *Dimitri Donskoi* met the first swells of the Baltic. He felt happy and contented, secure in the knowledge that his master's safety had been well taken care of.

Yes, all these people felt secure now, and they were all quite wrong. The life of Michael Kapitza didn't depend on guns or guards or security arrangements, but on Tania Vitgeft. Old Tania who had not only foretold his death, but left a legacy. Two faded letters, with which Florrie Bond was hoping to build up her boyfriend's business.

CHAPTER TEN

Tom Valley glanced across his desk towards the windows of his shop to make sure that no one was watching him from the street. Then he opened the top drawer. As always, the syringe lay in its little velvet case, ready and waiting to save life. He filled it slowly, rolled back his sleeve, and forced home the needle, seeing the metal sliver creep under his skin, but feeling no pain as he pressed the plunger. After ten years the nerves seemed to have grown immune to those tiny pinpricks. He withdrew it quickly as he saw Florrie turn into the doorway. She knew all about his condition, but he still hated anybody seeing it.

"Hullo, sweet, they been making you work overtime again?" He got up from the desk and kissed her lightly, pulling down his sleeve as he did so. "I'd almost begun to give you up."

"No, no overtime tonight, Tom." Florrie followed him into the little flat behind the shop. It had been a very nice flat when he'd first moved in, but now it was a shambles. The contents of the shop had overflowed into it. Books lay everywhere, piled on the chairs and tables and stacked in unsteady heaps against every wall.

"I'm late because I've been doing a bit of work on your behalf, darling." She pushed a heavy volume of the *Shorter Oxford Dictionary* off the seat of an armchair and sat. "You know that house in Benham Grove the department were interested in? I can't tell you why, of course, but when I went through the inventory I noticed that there were a lot of books which are to be handed over to the local auctioneers. I've been over there and made a list of them for you."

"Did you indeed?" Tom smiled. He felt much better just looking at her. She really was the girl for him, he decided. If he could only get his business on a proper footing, he'd ask her to marry him tomorrow. "Were they any good?"

"No, I don't think they were much good, though one or two might interest you." She opened her bag and pulled out the letters, not giving them to him at once, but holding them out like a fan in her hand.

"But the books aren't the important thing. It's these letters that I want you to look at. They were in an envelope stuck in the back of a copy of Semenoff's *Rasplata*. No, I'm not going to tell you what I think they may be, in case I'm completely wrong and you'll laugh at me. Just have a look for yourself and say what you think. You read German, don't you?"

"Yes, a little. And I won't laugh at you. I had a thorough training and I never laugh about manuscripts." He took them from her and switched on a lamp above the desk, frowning slightly as he did so. His late employer, Julius Rosen, had been very definite about manuscript material and his theme song had stuck in Tom's mind: "Never dismiss anything without checking it, Tommy boy. However busy you are, however unimportant you think it is, always check it carefully. In ninety-nine cases out of a hundred it will be junk, of course—a forgery, a printed facsimile—but there's always the one case, so go through it, son." Julius's hands had waved in emphasis as he gave that advice, and his face had crinkled into a thousand folds like the skin of a tortoise.

"And once I made a mistake, Tommy, a bad mistake. A long time ago it is now, but I still don't forget it. When I had the shop in Blackheath a man came and showed me a bundle of letters he wanted to sell. He didn't know anything about them, except that they were nineteenth-century, and neither did I. Written in a tiny cramped hand they was, and I couldn't make out the signature. I told the man they were no use to me and he went and sold them to Ernest Clarke of the Putney Vale Bookshop. Ten pounds, old Ernie paid for 'em; just ten pounds for eight letters. And do you know what he sold 'em for later, Tommy? Six thousand quid he got, because those letters I hadn't even bothered to check had been written by Emily Brontë. Never let me hear of you turning away manuscript material without going through it, son."

Tom Valley's eyes were very thoughtful as he laid the first page under the lamp and stared at the lines of Gothic script: "London, July 2nd 1882. *Mein Lieber* Fred, Yes, as I told you before, it would be most pleasant if Wedde's plan for a really scientific socialist journal could come about. In that way we could expose the utter ignorance of the university gentlemen and educate the minds of the general public, both working-class bourgeois . . ."

"Yes," he said. "I know who you think may have written these, but it's not possible, darling. Finds like that don't come up any more." He forced his voice to sound cautious and disinterested, but his hand shook slightly as he turned to the next page.

"*Mein Leiber* Fred . . . by chance I have found in a second-hand shop a *Report and Evidence on Scottish Tenant Rights*, House of Lords Issue, 1849. This should prove a most valuable find . . ."

Yes, that was the man's style all right, and the name "Wedde" rang a bell too. He got up from his desk and pulled a volume of an encyclopaedia from the shelf, feeling a prickle of sweat on his forehead as he did so. Yes, here it was: "Wedde,

Johannes (1840–95), Social Democrat. One of the original founders of the newspapers, *Hamburg Echo* and *Burgerseitung*. Expelled from Germany 1887."

But could it be genuine? Could this be the lucky break that all of them dreamed about, but so few ever found? Old Julius Rosen had had his chance and missed it, but others had done better. Norman Mayne of the Flaxman Bookshop, for instance, recognizing a seventeenth-century textbook as Robert Boyle's *Skeptical Chemist* and then, as he flicked through it, making out marginal notes by Sir Isaac Newton; Bertie Clyde picking up a battered sailing manual and seeing the signature of Horatio Nelson staring out at him from the flyleaf. But would he, Tom Valley, ever be given a chance to reach that dream—the unexpected jackpot which gave the job meaning? Somehow he felt in his bones that it was impossible. This was merely a printed facsimile, or a copy made by some eccentric with dishonest motives or too much time on his hands. He would be the laughing-stock of the trade if he ever made his hopes public.

All the same—he stared at the last letter: "I would be glad if you would give me your opinions on policy before the general council meeting on Wednesday [this time I hope we shall be without the unwelcome presence of reporters] ..."

"Yes," he said, looking up at Florrie. "The style seems right, as far as I can remember. The dates and phraseology fit, but I can't make out the signature. If only there were a set of facsimiles in the shop! Let's see what they would be worth if they were genuine." He pulled over a run of *Book Auction Records* and turned to the supplements which contained the sale prices of documents and manuscripts. He was almost certain that a similar letter had come up in the fifties.

1951—'52—'53—January, February, March. Yes, here it was. Sold at Sutherland's in Bond Street. One and a half pages, two hundred and five words, verified as genuine by the manuscript department of the British Museum. Property of the late Sir Basil Spain. Bought by I. K. Valinin, Esq., for £900.

Nine hundred! He made no attempt to conceal his excitement now. Nine hundred pounds for just one letter and he had two of them! They must be fakes, though. His luck wasn't good enough to let them be genuine. He slipped the letters between two sheets of cardboard and put a rubber band round them, staring across at Florrie as he did so.

"Well, sweet," he said, "let's keep our fingers crossed, because I'm right out of my depth now. All the same, if they are genuine, we're in the chips, so let's go and consult an expert." His hand started to reach out for the telephone, but even as he did so he knew it was useless. It was Saturday evening and Julius Rosen was a pious man who wouldn't break the Sabbath by answering it. They'd just have to go round to his flat and dig him out. Julius wouldn't be pleased about that, but to hell with him. He'd done the old boy enough favours in the past. Besides, he felt that if he didn't know about those letters soon he'd go crazy. He pushed them into his pocket and stood up. They almost seemed to burn his hand as he touched them.

Julius Rosen wasn't at all pleased to see his visitors. Very slowly and cautiously, as though there might be a squad of SS men lurking on the other side, he pulled open his door and blinked out into the corridor. He was very small, very old, with oddly bright and childlike eyes which didn't seem to belong to his wizened face; and under his skull-cap a rim of white hair stood out like a halo. His general appearance was strangely sinister. A musty, malevolent gnome from one of the Grimms' grimmer fairy stories, waiting to ensnare the unsuspecting traveller and lead him to his doom.

"Tommy—Tommy Valley and his young lady it is." His voice, a medley of accents picked up in half a dozen European capitals, contained annoyance and deep sadness. "And what brings you here at this time and day, son?"

"Hullo, Mr. Rosen." Tom gave no smile of greeting, for he knew it would merely increase Julius's displeasure. "I'm very sorry to bother you, but may we come in for a moment? I'm desperate for your opinion on something."

"Desperate! Desperate, you say! So desperate that you can't respect an old friend's privacy any more. All right then, come in if you must. Five minutes I shall give you—no more." He shook his head sadly and led them down a little dark passage. The room at the end of it was completely shelved from wall to ceiling and the books had overflowed from the shelves and stood in great ramparts around a desk, giving it the look of the nerve centre of some military outpost surrounded by fortifications.

"But listen to them, Tommy, just listen to them." Through the ceiling above could be heard the faint strains of Eartha Kitt singing about money. "My daughter Leah, that is. One year ago she marries that boy from Camberwell I was telling you about. Nice boy he seems, too, at first, reporter on the newspapers and very cultural—so Mrs. Joseph lets them have the flat above me. And what do they do? They play music—all the time they play music. Such music they play! Listen to it, my dears." His teeth made a sharp clocklike noise against the echo of Miss Kitt's chocolate rich voice.

"And now what is this opinion you're so desperate for, Tommy?"

"I've got a couple of letters I want you to look at, Mr. Rosen. I don't know if they're genuine, but—"

"But you think they may be important, eh?" Curiosity and injured piety mingled in Julius's face. "And you're a bright boy, Tommy. You know I like looking at manuscript material, and you also know that on this day I can't talk business or try to cut myself in on a deal, though there's nothing to stop me giving advice to a friend—even a *goy* friend.

"All right, five minutes you can have, as I said. Sit down if you can find somewhere, Tommy. You too, my dear." His youthful eyes flickered over Florrie as though she were a valuable piece of bric-a-brac Tom had picked up for a song.

"And now let's see these letters which you think may be all

right." He lowered himself cautiously into a chair behind his desk and switched on a green-shaded light.

"Yes, let's have a look." He slipped off the rubber band, laid the cardboard sheets on one side, and squinted at the first page. There was no excitement in his face yet, but he breathed a little deeper as he did so, rubbing a thin ink-stained finger across the bridge of his nose. A nose for a deal—a finger in the pie—make me an offer and no hard feelings. The five minutes he had promised were up when at last he looked at Tom again.

"Well, son, I know who you think may have written these, but don't let's count any chickens just yet. . . . What's that you say? A hundred to one against them being genuine? No, in my opinion, much more like a thousand to one. But let's make sure." He pulled over a box with an electric light bulb inside it, and laid a page on its glass top.

"Yes, this should tell me a little more." He lifted his magnifying glass and stared down at the glowing paper. "Well, at least it's not a printed facsimile. No ridges or type smears that I can see. This was written with a broad steel pen, and the nib had been buckled with too much pressure. That's something in our favour, anyway. If these are genuine you could start to be a rich boy, Tommy. But just hand me that set of facsimiles on the shelf beside you. On the right it should be.

"Thank you." Rosen thumbed through the book, grunting slightly as he found the reference, and laid it beside the lamp. "Yes, yes, so far so good. If it's a forgery it's a very clever one. Look at those cramped *t*'s and the way he's sloped the capitals. The ink seems all right, too—no ox gall mixed in to make it look old. Yes, a rich man you could be, son. Remember your old friends when you are.

"But the paper! No, I don't like the paper." He sniffed at it, ran his hand gently across it, and then stared through the glass again. "The date is about right, but it's expensive—too expensive. Very good quality handmade rag paper, and by all accounts our man was poor in those days. Good ink, too. Contains a lot of dextrin, as you can see from the highlights. Why should our man go and throw his money away on luxuries like that?"

"You mean it is a fake?" As he listened, all Tom's hopes seemed to come crashing down. There would be no jackpot for him this time. All he'd get would be a piece of old Julius's mind for disturbing his Sabbath and not learning the trade properly.

"I didn't say that, boy, not yet at least. All I said was that he used expensive writing materials. And why not? Perhaps some rich lady supporter gave 'em to him for a birthday present. But let me get on."

Rosen turned to the last page. Even as he did so he stiffened. His little body seemed to stretch and grow as taut as a wire, and there was not merely interest in his face, but a great glow of excitement. Centuries might have rolled back and he could have been standing beside Joshua looking at the Promised Land for the first time.

"But I've seen you somewhere before, my dear," he said. "I know you, don't I?" As he bent over the faded paper he could have been talking to a living person. "Once somebody showed you to me.

"Yes, listen to this, Tommy, what the man writes at the bottom of the page. 'The only good thing that may come of the war between France and Prussia is that the French need a tragic lesson in order to restore their manhood.' Yes, I remember that sentence. Where did you get these letters, son?"

"I got them, Mr. Rosen. They belonged to a woman named Tania Vitgeft who died last year." In spite of her better judgment Florrie's words came bubbling out. She wasn't looking at Julie, but at Tom. His face was set in a mask of complete dejection, and she knew exactly what he would be thinking. Julius had remembered that particular sentence and it proved the letters to be worthless fakes, laboriously copied from some printed collection. In a few minutes they would be sent on their way with a good deal of scorn poured on her find.

"Vitgeft—Tania Vitgeft. A Russian name, an uncommon

one too, but it rings me no bell at all. All the same, I've seen this letter somewhere before. Look how he's let the ink run a little here, and how the last line is cramped, as though he wanted to finish off on that page. Now, just where was it?" Rosen's forehead almost seemed to be cracking in his effort to concentrate.

"Ah yes, yes, I've got you, my dear. Silver had you!" He switched off the lamp and beamed in triumph. "You remember old Adrian Silver, Tommy?"

"Yes, I knew him slightly." Tom recalled a musty shop off Clapham Common presided over by another gnome who looked very like Julius Rosen. Adrian Silver had lived by selling junk, but he also collected manuscript material which he steadfastly refused to sell, stating that it was an insurance policy for his old age. An old age he never reached. When he was sixty he had married a lady thirty years his junior and died a few months later. The day after his funeral the widow had reopened the shop, with a row of boxes containing the precious manuscripts laid out on the table and marked two guineas each.

"Yes, of course you knew him, son. The old fool, the stupid brainless old fool. Wonderful stuff he had there, and he never told that bitch of a woman what it was worth. She just threw it away to the public without giving the Trade a chance to make her an offer." There was a gleam of fury in Julius's eyes, for like every dealer he hated the thought of the public getting a bargain.

"And these letters belonged to Silver?"

"Yes, Adrian had this one all right, like I'm telling you. I remember him showing it to me. Six or seven years ago it must have been, just before he died. He'd got its full history, too, and was prepared to swear it was genuine." He looked up and smiled at Florrie. "What did you pay for it, my dear, if you don't mind me asking?"

"I haven't paid anything yet, Mr. Rosen. I told the owners— the trustees of Vitgeft's estate—that I'd make them an offer if I found something was worth anything." As Florrie turned away from his grinning face, something had begun to stir in her mind. It had nothing to do with the money which would enable Tom to marry her, and nothing to do with the prestige which the letters would bring to his business. It was the thought of Tania Vitgeft that troubled her. Old Tania, a browser in junk-shops who might easily have got her hands on such letters, but also a member of a fanatical group of anti-Communists. If she had bought them from Silver's widow and sold them quickly, it was understandable. But to hide them away in an envelope stuck into the covers of a book on naval history—to keep them for years! It was about as unlikely as a pious Catholic concealing the works of Martin Luther under her bed.

"Did you now, my dear?" Rosen's voice rasped into her thoughts. "Very honest of you, and very wise. You've got a nice bright girl there, Tommy boy. See that you treat her well." He gave a final glance at the signature at the foot of the letter and replaced the cardboard covers and the rubber band.

"Yes, all quite genuine. I can swear to that, for Adrian Silver wasn't a man to make mistakes in his own line, whatever he did in other things. It's a lucky couple you are, my dears. When did another letter like these last come up now? Yes, 'fifty-three or 'four I think it was, and the owner got nearly a thousand quid for it. I'm pleased for you, Tommy. Little Tommy Valley who came to work for me when he was just a kid who couldn't even tell calf from morocco." He got up and handed Tom the packet—a grinning fairy-tale gnome giving the youngest son the magic sword that would win him his princess and a kingdom. As though in blessing, Miss Kitt's voice above them ground to an end and was replaced by a raucous calypso.

"And be sure that you ask a good price for these, boy—a very good price indeed. As I see it, there's only one possible customer, but he's a rich man. Richer than Ford, or Mr. Getty, or all the Rothschilds put together. And now I want you to leave me alone, please." He grinned at Tom again, patted Florrie on the shoulder as though complimenting a clever child, and led them to the door. As he pulled it open, his eyes ran lovingly over the little cardboard packet in Tom's hand.

"Yes, my dears, you've really done it this time, I think. A find like everybody in the Trade dreams of, like we dream of picking up a First Folio or an original edition of *Alice in Wonderland*, so be sure and ask a good price. You'll get it all right. I haven't any doubts about that. No, the Soviet Government won't haggle about what they pay for two quite genuine letters to Friedrich Engels from Karl Marx."

CHAPTER ELEVEN

From the moment that he had called for her at the farm, Sophia Robinson had disliked Igor Trubenoff. After five minutes in his company she feared him.

She sat as far away from him as the car seat allowed, studying him with occasional quick glances. She remembered his type from a dozen school textbooks. A suit which had probably cost more than Mike earned in two months, the thin cynical face grinning out under the hairless skull, and eyes which looked as though they had seen everything that the world could offer and discarded most of it as worthless, though sometimes amusing. This was the real enemy that they had told her about when she was a child. The aristocrat, the traitor who had escaped from the wrath of Mother Russia and now plotted in dark places to enslave her children again. Even the smile and the little bow he had given her as she opened the door for him had made her feel that. Not the smile of a friend or even an employer, but of a master tossing a few kopeks to some deserving serf.

"And you are sure you understand the arrangements, Mrs. Robinson?" Quite oblivious of the effect he was creating, Trubenoff swung the car onto the Chelmsford by-pass and smiled again. When he had first been told that he was to act

as her escort, he had felt extremely put out; the senior exec-
utive who has been asked to take on humbler duties during
an epidemic or an office crisis. Even when Kirk had explained
the position to him he had not been completely mollified.
Since he had seen her for himself, however, he had changed
his mind. The woman was obviously in a highly critical state
of nerves and, if she was to do what they wanted, would need
somebody responsible at her side.

"Yes, they are clear enough, thank you." Sophia Robinson
turned away from him and looked out of the window. The
countryside had changed completely during the last few miles.
Instead of the long flat fields there were little wooded slopes,
and the churches were low and squat and quite different from
the tall ship-like buildings that dominated the horizons of the
farm. Poor Mike, she thought, as she remembered them. Poor
Mike and the kids. They were quite ignorant of what she was
doing and they'd get a shock when they came back from Bury
market and found she wasn't there. All the same, the note and
the cheque she'd left on the kitchen table should soften the
blow a little. Whatever happened, the mortgage would be
taken care of.

"Yes, I know what I'm expected to do. Colonel Danilenko
gave me very detailed instructions. I am to pose as a reserve
interpreter and stand beside you on the launch. The cruiser is
due to anchor off Southend at six o'clock and we will meet it
there. When Kapitza comes aboard I have to see if I recognize
one of his bodyguard who might have been at Koshuba."

"That's it, Mrs. Robinson. Not a very difficult way of earning three thousand pounds, I think."

"No, perhaps not." She lowered her eyes slightly. If only he
understood, she thought. If only the bastard really knew the
price that would have to be paid for her simple service. Would
that take the smile from his cynical, well-bred features? No,
probably not. Men like Trubenoff would still smile if they saw
their world split apart.

"But may I ask you a personal question please, Mr.

Trubenoff?" She hated pronouncing the Russian name, knowing that it would tell what she was—a slum dweller from the
back streets of Leningrad. "Your family in Russia—were they
landowners?"

"Landowners? That's a strange question, Mrs. Robinson!"
Trubenoff looked away from her as he slid the car past a lorry
and accelerated. "Yes, I suppose you could call them that.
My father was an officer in the Imperial Russian Navy and he
owned a small estate near Odessa. After the Reds defeated
Denikin, he managed to escape to France. Like many émi-
grés, he drove a Paris taxi. He wasn't very good at it, I'm afraid.
Missed his gears and brakes on a hill in Montmartre and ended
up against one of those metal cylinders they cover with adver-
tisements.

"A funny old boy. I remember going to see him in hospital.
Though the doctor had told him he was dying, he'd insisted on
keeping his monocle screwed in, and he'd got a nurse to comb
his beard. When I came into the ward he smiled and tried to
raise his hand in greeting, but it seemed that the muscles were
paralyzed and he could only move it a couple of inches. I asked
him if he was badly hurt and he smiled again. 'Yes, pretty badly,
Igor Nikolayevitch,' he said. 'In fact I'm done for, but don't let
it worry you. I always knew that I should meet my end in some
such ridiculous manner.'"

"And then he died?" There was no sympathy in Sophie's
voice. She felt that those were just the kind of cynical, decadent words that people like Trubenoff's father always did die
with.

"Yes, he died. I left France soon after that and went to work
for the English—against my own people. Just as you are doing
now, Mrs. Robinson."

"Yes, just like I'm doing." Though the day was warm she felt
a sudden stab of cold as she answered him. "You are employed
by the British Intelligence, Mr. Trubenoff, not the L.W.R.?"

"The League of White Russians?" Without warning
Trubenoff threw back his head and laughed. It was a manly,

aristocratic and completely sham laugh. The relic of another age, handed down across the years, and it made her think of champagne suppers in heavily curtained rooms that smelled of incense. Gypsies dancing to balalaikas, and officers' epaulets glinting. If Trubenoff had had four hands and bright green hair he wouldn't have seemed more alien to her than he did with that sudden burst of aristocratic sham laughter.

"No, I'm afraid I am not part of Colonel Danilenko's monkey show," he said. "I am merely an employee of the British Government, a watchdog who does exactly what they tell me to do. At the moment my charge is to see that our fellow countryman, Michael Kapitza, remains in good health while he is over here."

"But all the same you believe in him, don't you? In Danilenko, I mean. You must believe that what he has told you is correct. That one of Kapitza's bodyguard is an assassin who will make an attempt on his life in London."

"I believe that it *may* be correct, Mrs. Robinson, nothing more. For all I know, the whole story may be an invention of the good Colonel's to make his organization seem important. All the same, there is no harm in assuming that Danilenko has told us the exact truth and acting on it. That is why you are being paid a great deal of money for a few hours' work." He slowed the car before a sign pointing towards Southend, and turned off onto a white concrete highway. Through the open windows came a faint smell of the sea.

"And that reminds me about something." Trubenoff took his eyes off the road for a moment and glanced at her. "As Danilenko admits himself, the information he gave us was very incomplete. All that Durkin, his contact in Berlin, could tell him was that the assassin had once been an inmate at Koshuba Camp. The supposition is that he was a guard or official there, but personally I wonder. I think it is probably much more likely that he was not a guard, but a prisoner."

"A prisoner! I don't understand you."

"Don't you? Don't you really, Mrs. Robinson?" Trubenoff shook his head slightly. "You know more about it than I do, of course, but wasn't the main speciality of Koshuba thought control—brain washing, in popular terms? Isn't it possible that the person we hope you will recognize may not be a well-paid professional killer or a dedicated fanatic, but merely a piece of human wreckage who does what he is told to do without thought or understanding, just as this car stops when I move my foot?" He braked to allow a party of schoolchildren to march slowly and pompously over a crossing.

"Yes, I suppose it is possible." Sophie looked out at the streets of Southend. Hotels and boarding houses and cafés. "Room to Let" and "Coaches Welcome" signs in windows, and the names of holidays over doors "Balmoral . . . Tintagel . . . Costa Brava . . . Côte d'Azur." She could hardly read them because of another sign which was spreading out behind her eyes. A huge red and black sign, towering up over the cheerless countryside of the Urals with words that read, "C.C.C.P., Koshuba 27," but really meant, "Abandon Hope All Ye Who Enter Here."

And behind the sign there had been barbed wire, and rows of little huts which were hot in the summer and stale with human sweat, but in the winter so cold that the bodies huddled together for warmth. There had been lights, too, in some of those huts. Great blinding lights with faceless voices behind them. Voices which always sounded exactly the same, and always asked the same questions. "Don't you understand that the British sailor, Michael Robinson, is a spy who made you betray your country? How often did you meet him— What did you tell him— How much did he pay you— How often did you have intercourse with him— How often— How much— How many times— Anything else— Anything else— Anything else?" The voices were very loud and clear above the sound of the car, and she suddenly seemed to feel that those years at Koshuba were the only part of her life that had really existed. Everything else was a dream.

"Yes, I suppose he might have been a prisoner." She fought to tear the image out of her mind. "They did try brain washing sometimes. In my case they failed."

"But of course they failed, my dear. If they had succeeded, you would hardly be sitting beside me now." Trubenoff raised his hand from the steering-wheel and lightly patted her arm. The gesture was about as impersonal as if he were patting a strange dog.

"No, all I am suggesting is that there is a possibility that the man may not have been a guard, but a prisoner. I may be quite wrong, of course, but please be on the lookout for any face at all that you think you may have seen at the camp.

"But we're almost there it seems." He smiled out at the sea-front which was opening up before them. It was probably always crowded during the summer, he thought, but today it was bursting. Cars and buses lay in a glittering, unbroken line along the curb, and he could make out the masts and funnels of pleasure-steamers tied up against the pier. And everywhere there was densely packed humanity. Thousands of people—half a million perhaps, and all of them were waiting to see the arrival of Kapitza's warship. She was still four hours and a hundred and twenty miles away, sweeping in across the swell, but already the people of England were massing on the pier and promenades in the hope of catching a glimpse of the man she carried. Michael Kapitza, the little bearded hope for peace, who at this moment would probably be sitting in his stateroom and discussing final arrangements with his staff. Some of those people would be normal holiday-makers, of course. A few would have come from idle curiosity, but the vast majority would be there to cheer. He shuddered inwardly at the thought of their rage if anything went wrong, as it easily might. Yes, very easily might. Unless he, Igor Nikolayevitch Trubenoff, played his cards correctly, Kapitza would be dead meat before he reached Westminister Steps.

"Yes, here we are." He turned the car into the parking-lot beside the customs house. "This is where you put on the disguise we promised you, and we have a final briefing from the naval officer in command of the launch.

"But first I think that there is an important piece of ritual we should perform. We've just got time to walk across to that public house over the road and wish ourselves luck with a drink. Believe me, I think we're going to need all the luck we can get." He got out of the car and walked around to open the door for her.

"No, Sophie Petrovna," he said. "You don't like me, do you? You think that I'm a very nasty piece of work indeed. Though you, yourself, are a British subject now, you feel that I am a survivor of an evil and decadent system which should have died years ago. Well, maybe you're right. All the same, for today at least, we have to work together, so let me buy you a drink before we start."

"Very well, if that's what you wish." Sophie climbed out beside him, her handbag feeling like a lead weight as she pulled it after her. She stared up at the pale sky, the same wide sky that lay over Mike's farm, with the same flat streaks of cloud drifting in from the east. But here it seemed quite different. It lacked something. They had almost reached the door of the public house before she realized what was missing from the sky. Not the tall churches standing out like ships on its horizons, or the fields spreading like fans below it, but the little gold and silver lines that crossed it like lattice-work. The vapour trails of the American bombers—vapour trails widening.

CHAPTER TWELVE

"Easy now, lad, just take it nice and easy. Not much farther to go and we mustn't break a valve at this stage of the proceedings." Mr. Triggs backed into Kirk's office waving on his assistant, an undersized youth of sixteen who was almost hidden under an enormous television set.

"Right, that's fine, Arch. Set her down over there and gently does it." He watched the boy lower his burden with a resounding crash, then pulled out a handkerchief, wiping his face as though it were he himself who had been carrying the set.

"Well, that's it, Miss Bond. All present and correct, though it's been warm work getting it up here." He beamed at Florrie with the air of a modest man who would still appreciate a compliment. "Yes, you gave us quite a job getting hold of a set at such short notice. It's a lucky thing we happened to have a friend at court, as the saying goes."

"I know that, Mr. Triggs, and I'm sure General Kirk will be most grateful to you. It was only this afternoon that he decided to watch Kapitza's arrival from here instead of going down to Southend."

"Quite so. And we'll make sure that he has a good picture." Triggs tucked away his handkerchief and glowered at Arch.

"Well, come on, lad, don't stand about there doing nothing. Get a move on and couple her up. See that you have your earth connection good and tight and we'll put the aerial up on the mantelpiece; well out of the way where the old gentleman can't go knocking into it.

"Right. Now, let's see what we've got." With the deliberation of a scientist about to throw a moon rocket in orbit Mr. Triggs turned a switch and moved back a few paces.

"No, no, not too bad, though perhaps we could do with a little more focus. Ah, that's better, isn't it? Now just move the aerial a little more to the right, will you? Yes, that's it. Most satisfactory. General Kirk should have a very good clear picture. We've done a nice job at such short notice, though we say it ourselves."

"I'm sure you have, Mr. Triggs. And now, if you've finished, I'm afraid I've got rather a lot of work to do." This was not entirely correct, but Florrie had a great deal on her mind and desperately wanted to be alone with her own thoughts before Kirk came back to the office.

"Yes, we're all finished now, miss, but there's one thing we must warn you about. If the General doesn't want a breakdown in his viewing, on no account must that—that—" He glowered at Kirk's electric fire as though at a loss for words to describe it. "On no account must that contraption be turned on full. From what we've heard, the circuit will be carrying a pretty heavy load this evening. Miss Hamble's decoding machine will be in use as well as—"

"But this is quite abominable, Mr. Triggs." Florrie frowned at him. "You told me yourself that there was no danger of blowing a fuse unless all the fires on this floor were switched on. I should have thought that was pretty unlikely in midsummer."

"Ah, but that was before we started to check the wiring, Miss Bond. We made a quick inspection yesterday, just after Mr. Virgo's new Veri-typer was installed, and a very poor flimsy job we found it to be—like so much of the stuff that's being done these days. We'd never have passed it, of course, but it seems that this floor was rewired just before we took over the building." He wagged a gnarled finger at her.

"No, until we've had the opportunity of going over the building, we've put in weaker fuses which won't stand the load of the General's machine."

"It's them Turks what's responsible, miss." Triggs' diminutive assistant stopped gathering his tools together and scowled up at her. "'Arf the botched jobs today are done by them. Why, my dad says that the bastards never even invented the wheel."

"The Turks!" Florrie could only stare at him in amazement. "What on earth have they got to do with it?"

"Archie means the Irish, Miss Bond. And you watch your language when there's ladies present, lad." Triggs made another slight adjustment on the set and then switched it off as though satisfied.

"The lower sections of the community often refer to the Irish as Turks, though we've never discovered why. The name seems to fit them, however. A rough, uncouth people they seem to be, without pride in honest work or skill at a craft. They come over here to pocket high wages and then hurry home to drink themselves to death in some miserable hovel on a bog. It wasn't so bad when they were merely employed as pick and shovel men, but now they seem to have spread into every branch of the building trade: masons, carpenters, steel erectors. Even electrical engineers we're sorry to say. A very bad state of affairs indeed.

"But you want to get on with your work, miss, and we'd best be off for a well-deserved cup of tea. Got your tools all present and correct, lad? Good.

"Now, don't you forget what we told you, Miss Bond. On no account must this fire of the General's be turned on full, till we've had time to check through the circuit."

"Yes, I'll remember, Mr. Triggs, and thank you for fixing up the television for us." Florrie watched him strut out of the room with Arch at a regulation three paces at his heels, and sat down at her desk.

The building seemed to be unnaturally quiet today, almost as though its bricks and girders were waiting for news of Kapitza's arrival. She glanced up at the big electric wall clock above the door. Four o'clock and very soon they would know if Danilenko's warning was correct. By now Trubenoff and Mrs. Robinson would have reached Southend. By now the Soviet cruiser would be less than sixty miles away, ploughing on across the North Sea at thirty knots, with the officers very smart in their full-dress uniforms, and the radio room humming with messages to England. Just sixty miles and they would know the truth. Fifty—forty—twenty miles. Somewhere on that ship, playing cards perhaps, reading, killing time, there would be a group of quietly dressed men with anonymous faces whose job it was to see that Kapitza lived. If Danilenko had told Kirk the truth, one of them would have another job as well and in his pocket would lie a little disguised gun that spat cyanide.

But God, she felt guilty! Great waves of guilt, as sour as sick-room sweat, seemed to wrap themselves round her. She had meant to tell Kirk about those Marx letters all day, but he had seemed so tense and preoccupied that she hadn't dared. It wasn't the fact of taking them that was important, of course. That didn't matter, for Tania Vitgeft had left no heir, and she had few scruples about a little sharp practice at the expense of the public trustee. Besides, it wasn't really stealing. Tom was going to show the letters to the Soviet Embassy in the hope that they would make him an offer, and then they would take them back to the house and replace them in the flap where she had found them. As soon as that was done he would make Hyde, Herod & Scott a good offer for the library and hope they would accept. Sharp practice maybe, but not stealing—not important at all. The important thing was to know why the letters should have been there in the first place.

Florrie got up and pulled a thick folder from the filing cabinet. It contained all the department knew about Tania Vitgeft and three pictures of her. The first was a passport photograph and it told nothing at all. It showed a face, a nose, two eyes and a rather bitter mouth, but nothing of their owner's personality. The second was better. It seemed to have been taken from a local newspaper and showed her walking down a street. A tall gaunt old woman with a hat that looked like a prop for a game of charades, a moth-eaten fur around her neck, and a dress that brushed the pavement. The face above the fur didn't look completely mad, but it certainly wasn't sane, and there was a hint of humourless fanaticism about it. The face of someone who could probably stand any torture, but would break down if she were laughed at. Florrie could imagine Tania Vitgeft striding into a police station and browbeating some Soviet deserter. She could also imagine her browsing among bric-a-brac shops and trying to beat down the salesmen: "Yes, I would like to have this clock, but only if you will take a little less for it. . . . This vase is quite nice, but I couldn't pay more than a pound. . . . This box of letters, Mrs. Silver? Would you be prepared to sell two of them separately?"

No, no, she just couldn't imagine that. Letters from the father of communism to his closest associate! That didn't fit in with what they knew of Vitgeft at all. It was as unlikely that she should collect them as it would be to find a staunch Daughter of the American Revolution hanging a picture of Benedict Arnold above her dressing table.

She turned to the last photograph and forced herself to look at it, for it had been taken after death—a long time after death. The face was like a turnip-lantern roughly carved by children, with the eyes shrunk to leather buttons and withered lips drawn back to show the blackened teeth. Tania Vitgeft had died a year ago and was buried, but as Florrie looked at the horrible picture she suddenly had the feeling that her mummified corpse had climbed out of its grave and was standing beside her trying to tell her the name of its killer. She had no theory, not even a hunch to go on, but a strong feeling that his name might somehow be hidden in those faded letters which Tom Valley was about to quote to the Soviet Embassy. She pushed the pictures away as the phone rang, and went back to the desk to answer it.

"Room Fifty-seven. Yes, Miss Bond here. Oh, it's you, Colonel Danilenko." She felt a wave of returning confidence at the sound of his rich reassuring voice.

"No, I'm afraid the General is still out, though he shouldn't be long. He asked me to give you a message. Would you come round here at about five-thirty and watch Kapitza's arrival with him on the television?"

"Did he indeed?" she heard Danilenko ask. "He's not gone down to Southend himself then? Well, I hope he knows what he's doing, because it's up to you people now. We've given you all the help we can, and Kapitza's safety is in your hands." A chair creaked as though Danilenko was shifting his bulk to a more comfortable position, and Florrie could imagine the room he sat in. Though she had never been to the headquarters of the L.W.R. herself, Kirk had described it to her with much sneering detail: carved panelling, look-through mirrors, and an enormous oil painting of the Tzar and Tzarina above the oversized desk. "A damn stage set," Kirk had called it, but she thought that it was probably very impressive. She was beginning to think that everything about Danilenko was impressive.

"Very well then, Miss Bond," he said. "Please tell the General that I'll look forward to seeing him about five thirty. By the way, have you heard if my protégée, Mrs. Robinson, has arrived at Southend yet?"

"She should have done, Colonel, but if you'd hold on for a moment, I'll make sure." She went through into the outer office and consulted the list of incoming calls.

"Yes, sir. Mr. Trubenoff rang through a few minutes ago and they're there now."

"Good, then let's keep our fingers crossed. I'll be round at half past five."

"I'll tell General Kirk that, Colonel. Until this evening, then—" She started to say goodbye and then stopped. Though she hardly knew Danilenko, there was something in his personality that made her want to confide in him.

"Colonel Danilenko, please don't think I'm impertinent, but I'd like to ask you a personal question. Just how well did you know Princess Vitgeft?"

"How well did I know her!" She could almost picture the flicker of irritation running across his face—boredom and weariness at all female curiosity. "I suppose I knew her as well as anybody, but that's saying very little. I doubt if anybody really knew old Tania well. But why do you ask, Miss Bond?"

"It's rather difficult to explain, Colonel. It's just that something cropped up a couple of days ago and it's been worrying me, though I don't really know why." She glanced at the clock again. Kirk was due back at any moment and he wouldn't be pleased to find her chatting to Danilenko. Her next words came out in a rush.

"Colonel Danilenko, what would you say if I told you that Vitgeft was in possession of two manuscript letters from Karl Marx to Engels?"

For a moment, he didn't say anything. For perhaps ten seconds there was silence on the line. When he spoke again, his voice was still polite, bored, and indifferent.

"I think I would say that you were pulling my leg, Miss Bond. You don't honestly expect me to believe that the police found such letters, do you?"

"No, Colonel, the police didn't find them, or if they did, they didn't know what they were. I found the letters and I think I'd like to tell you about it." With her eyes still on the clock she told him. She told him everything. How she had gone round to the house to list the books, and how she had found the letters in the back cover of *Rasplata*. How she had shown them to Tom and what Tom intended to do with them.

"I see. And I'm very glad that you've confided in me, Miss Bond, though it seems that you've been rather a naughty girl. I gather General Kirk merely gave you permission to look at the books, not to remove anything from the house." The indifference seemed to be leaving Danilenko's voice now.

"But that's not my affair, and there may be a dozen reasons why Tania had these letters. She once told me that she collected Russian naval history as her father was killed at Tsushima, and she could have bought the book without knowing they were hidden in it. She also could have spotted what they were and hoped to sell them at an enormous profit—like your Mr. Valley is intending to do. She may have merely wanted to conceal them."

"To conceal them? I don't understand, Colonel."

"You should, if you try to consider Tania's character for a moment. Though she was a member of our movement and an old friend, I would never pretend that she was completely sane. Her fanaticism—her hatred of communism—was not based on any rational beliefs, but on mania. I suppose you know that she had been raped by Red soldiers during the Revolution?"

"No, I didn't know that. But what are you trying to tell me, Colonel? You say that she might want to *conceal* the letters."

"I am trying to show you how Tania's mind might have worked if she came across such letters. Two genuine letters from Karl Marx, a man whom she thought of as a kind of anti-Christ, responsible for all the evils of the world. She might destroy them, but she might prefer to lock them away. To hide them in the dark and gloat over the fact that nobody would ever see them. If Tania Vitgeft had been born in another age, I think she could well have been burned as a witch, and witches collect possessions of people they hate, don't they? Fingernail parings, locks of hair, pictures. Though Marx died a long time ago, I think Tania might have enjoyed the thought of having a couple of his letters in her possession— But please hold the line for a moment, will you?" He broke off and Florrie knew that his hand was cupped over the mouthpiece of the phone as though he were talking to someone beside him.

"All the same," he said when he came on again, "I'm not very happy about what you've told me. Though there may be a dozen quite innocent reasons for those letters being in Tania's house, there could be another reason which isn't innocent at all, but extremely sinister. No, I won't talk about it on the phone and, for your own sake, I wouldn't mention the letters to General Kirk. He won't be pleased with what you've done and I don't think you should disturb him while he's preoccupied with Kapitza's arrival. Let's just keep it to ourselves for the time being, though there's one thing you must do. On no account should Mr. Valley be allowed to show the letters to the Soviet authorities till we're quite sure why Tania had them. Will you see to that at once, please?"

"Yes, of course, Colonel. I'll try to get in touch with him straightaway."

"You do that, Miss Bond. Do it just as soon as I've rung off." All at once Danilenko's voice sounded quite different. All the quiet urbanity had left it; it seemed harsh, brutal, almost threatening.

"On no account whatsoever must the Soviet Embassy be informed about these letters till we know exactly why they were in Tania Vitgeft's possession. On no account at all, Miss Bond. And, if you let me down, I'll make it my personal business to see that General Kirk breaks both you and Mr. Valley. I hope you understand me, Miss Bond."

"Yes, I understand, Colonel." Florrie heard the line go dead. She didn't lower the phone for a moment, but sat holding it in her hand and staring across the room. She had not the slightest idea what Danilenko meant, but the sudden flaring brutality in his voice had stunned her. Then at last, almost as though the effort were too much for her, she started to dial Tom's number. The busy tone sounded like the opening bars of some very modern and rather macabre symphony.

CHAPTER THIRTEEN

But Florrie was too late. Tom Valley had already been in touch with the Soviet Embassy. Sharp at nine-thirty that morning he had rung them, and, though the place was obviously in turmoil with preparations for Kapitza's arrival, he had at last got through to the person he wanted.

It had taken him a long time, of course. A good ten minutes had been spent trying to explain himself to a harassed receptionist who seemed to know very little English, and this had been followed by a five-minute silence in which he thought he had been cut off. Then at last a switch had clicked and he heard the voice of somebody who claimed the unlikely name of Dr. Vasya Drozd.

But Dr. Drozd seemed knowledgeable and was obviously very interested. Tom could almost hear him bubbling with excitement as he explained what he had to sell.

"Yes, yes, indeed, Mr. Valley. Of course, my Government would wish to purchase such letters, providing they were genuine and you could give us proof of ownership. What you have told me is really most interesting. My friend, Professor Vodin, of the Marx-Engels Institute in Moscow, claims they have an almost complete collection of the correspondence. If your find is really what you say, this could take the wind right out of his sails—to use an English phrase." Tom felt a great hope for humanity as he heard that. Scholars were very much the same everywhere it seemed, and he could imagine a long and acrimonious correspondence taking place in *Pravda* just as it often did in the *Times* or *Herald Tribune*.

"But may I ask just how these letters came into your possession, Mr. Valley?"

"No, I'm afraid I'm not allowed to tell you that at the moment, Dr.—" Tom made a half-hearted attempt at the name, but it sounded as much like a stifled belch as anything else. "I'm selling them on behalf of a private collector who prefers to remain anonymous."

"Oh, I see." Drozd didn't sound as though he saw at all. "That is rather annoying, but doubtless he won't mind giving his name if we decide the letters are genuine. Now, I wonder if you would be kind enough to read through the text to me, Mr. Valley. Rather slowly, please, so that I can make a transcript.

"Yes, thank you—thank you very much indeed. Yes, they are interesting—very interesting in fact. The reference to the reporters put in brackets and the way he intersperses English words with the German are both typical of Marx's style. I would like to see these letters as soon as possible, Mr. Valley. I wouldn't be able to make you a definite offer myself, of course, as I'm merely the Embassy librarian and records keeper. All the same, if I'm assured they are genuine, I'd be very surprised if I couldn't persuade my colleagues at the Marx-Engels Institute to talk business. Yes, this will make old Vodin sit up with a jerk." A little chuckle of laughter sounded through the phone.

"Now, just how much are you asking for the letters, Mr. Valley?"

"I want three thousand two hundred." Tom doubled the last recorded price for such a letter.

"Do you, indeed! Pounds or dollars, Mr. Valley?" There was a slightly hopeful note in Drozd's voice as though he were expecting to make something for himself on the deal. It was cut short as Tom told him.

"I see, pounds, eh! A very large sum of money, Mr. Valley. All the same, my Government are generous payers when they want something, and they may very well go to three thousand.

"Now, when can I have a look at the letters? Oh no, no, please don't even think of bringing them here. That would

never do. You see at the moment things are completely—"
Though Drozd was doubtless a loyal and patriotic Soviet
citizen, he sounded extremely put out by the turmoil that
Kapitza's visit was causing the Embassy.

"What I suggest is that I come round and see you. No, I can't
manage today, I'm afraid, but what about tomorrow afternoon? Would three o'clock do? Good, then if you would just
give me your address, Mr. Valley, I'll look forward to seeing
you. And you will be careful with those letters, won't you?
If they are genuine it's a very wonderful find indeed and I'm
quite certain we will want to buy them."

"Don't worry, Doctor, I'll take good care of them. Goodbye
for the present then." Tom smiled down at the grey sheets of
paper as he replaced the phone. If Drozd really was an expert
on Marx material he would be able to pronounce them genuine after five minutes' examination. As soon as he had done so,
Florrie could return them to the Vitgeft house, and he would
ask Hyde, Herod & Scott for a private view of the books, and
make them a thumping offer for the lot. Not too thumping,
of course. There was no point in arousing their suspicions
that something of value was tucked away in the dusty shelves.
Judging from Florrie's list, a hundred pounds would be a safe
offer, and one which they could hardly refuse.

Yes, three thousand, just like that! He could use that sort
of money all right, he decided, staring around his shop. It was
very quiet, even for a Monday, and he didn't suppose his assistant had taken a penny since she opened an hour ago. The
books on the shelves had a sad waiting look. Not a bad stock,
though—quite a nice stock really—painstakingly built up over
the years he had spent working for Julius Rosen and dreaming
of the day when he would start on his own. All the same, three
thousand pounds' worth of new blood would cheer it up considerably.

Yes, he'd take good care of those letters. They would stay
the night in his bank, and tomorrow Drozd would peer over
them with a glass and pronounce them quite genuine. It might

hurry things up, too, if he had a couple of photostats made right away and posted one to Drozd. Yes, he'd do that. Almost with a song in his heart he put the letters in his pocket and went out.

The *Dimitri Donskoi* was a brand new ship, only two months out of the builders' hands, and she made a fine sight with her black and grey paint, the lines of bunting strung between the towering funnels, and the Russian and British ensigns stiff at each mast. She'd made a good passage across the North Sea, and was dead on time. On the far horizon her lookouts could already make out a dark strip which was land, and a line of dots moving out from it.

"England." The *Donskoi's* captain pointed with his hand. "We've got you here on schedule, Comrade Minister."

"Yes, so you have." Kapitza nodded and turned to the woman who leaned against the rail beside him. "You see it, Sonia?"

"Yes, I see it, Michael." The woman smiled, but she didn't look up at him. Her worn peasant face bore an expression of wonder as she watched the approaching coastline. She had never been out of Russia in her life, and she felt as excited as a child on Christmas Eve as she watched the flat Essex shore. "England—journey's end, my dear."

"Journey's end? I wonder." Kapitza knew, though, that his wife was completely wrong. This was not the end for him, but the beginning. The first bastion to be entered—the first enemy to be made a friend. The real end of his journey would not be the Thames estuary, but the New York skyline. "All the same, a very happy birthday to you, my dear," he said.

And one day he would make that landfall. He knew that he would make it. Soon Nikita Khrushchev would retire, and when he did, he, Michael Kapitza, son of a drunken wood-cutter from Smolensk, was the only person who could take his place. On the day he did, the barriers would go down like paper screens, and the rat-race of bombs and rockets and madness would come to an end.

"My wife and I would like to thank you for a most pleasant journey, Captain Makaroff." His words were completely automatic; he was still preoccupied with his own thoughts. He remembered how his advisers had warned him against this visit. How General Malendin, head of the security forces, had stumped up and down his office, dragging his steel foot heavily on the carpet, and threatened to resign. "Listen to me for a moment, Michael Petrovitch," he had said, his scarred face twisting up into a frown which made it look like a devil-mask. "My old friend, don't you realize how many people there are who would like to kill you? And the point is that they daren't do so in Russia. Can't you see that this is the very opportunity they are waiting for, and they'll take it? If you make that journey to England, I just can't be held responsible for your safety."

Well, he'd given in last year and postponed the first visit, but this time he'd had to go, though he saw Malendin's point. He had enemies—lots of enemies. The old die-hard extremists who had been trained in the days of violence and would hang on to power till he broke them.

Some of those enemies were dead, of course. He remembered how Anton Beria had died as the bullets thudded into him. That tight oval face, which looked like a rubber inner tube stretched over the bone structure, staring down at his torn belly, and tears—yes, real tears—running under the rimless glasses as he watched the little fountain of blood and urine spurt through his fingers. Beria had been the most hated man in Russia, but at that moment he could have forgiven him anything except the sight of that rubber face weeping.

Yes, Beria was dead. And Lynov was dead—clawing at the walls and screaming for help under the typewriter cover they had tied over his face before dragging him out to the car. And Molotov was broken—expelled from the Party, with new names marking the villages and factories that had once been called after him.

Yes, most of them were dead or finished, but not all. Marshal Anydir, for example—Peter Felkesham—Admiral Radin—they all lived and prayed that he would die first. Paula Stein! No, he wouldn't think about her. Not about that blotched shapeless face which looked as though it had been moulded out of plasticine, with the bright eyes staring from it like beads.

No, he wouldn't think about his enemies today, but of his friends. He looked down onto the deck where most of his bodyguards were leaning on the rail and watching the approaching shore. Yes, all old friends whom he could trust completely and who had been with him for years. He smiled as he remembered Malendin's warning: "Once out of Russia they will try to shoot you down like a mad dog, and there is nothing I can do to stop them." Malendin was a stupid old busybody and quite wrong. With those men around him he could walk through the gates of hell and come back unscathed.

"I think this must be your welcoming committee." Captain Makaroff pointed westward. "Yes, British J Class frigates they seem to be." The line of dots had become ships now. Four little grey ships—rather a darker grey than the Russian cruiser, he noticed—leaping over the swell like dancers, their ensigns stiff in the breeze and their sirens whooping.

"Yes, very nice of them." Kapitza watched the frigates wheel in formation and take up their positions on either side of the *Donskoi*; then he looked at the estuary that was opening up before him. Flat, low coastlines dotted with little white houses and the hint of a town in the distance, a red lightship swaying to port of them, and all along the shore a cloud of yachts and small craft that looked as bright as confetti with their flags and bunting.

"Well, what is it now, Ivan?" He frowned impatiently as his secretary hurried across the bridge towards them with a folder in his hand. "Surely you haven't got more documents for me to sign? If this goes on you'll have to get a rubber stamp made."

"No, Minister, there's nothing for you to sign this time." Though the man was still in his twenties, his responsibilities had made him look almost middle-aged. He fussed over

Kapitza like an indulgent nannie with a delicate and extremely difficult child.

"I thought you might like to know that I've been on the radio again and settled those two points we wanted changed. The seating arrangements at the formal banquet tonight will be as you asked, and the visit to Buckingham Palace tomorrow will be three-quarters of an hour earlier."

"Tomorrow, Ivan?" Kapitza turned away from him as a signal gun started to boom out across the swell, and a fresh chorus of whoops came from the frigates. Already he could make out tiny figures waving on the yachts offshore. Not in forty years, he thought. No, not since the Revolution could a Russian statesman have had such a warm welcome from the British.

"Yes, tomorrow." He spoke very quietly. The wind was tugging at his grizzled beard and the evening sunlight glinting on his face. He laid an arm around his wife's shoulder and smiled at the narrowing estuary. As he did so, he suddenly seemed to see the Manhattan skyscrapers rising above it like a mirage.

"Tomorrow, Sonia. I wonder. Yes, tomorrow it won't be merely England, but the whole world."

CHAPTER FOURTEEN

By five o'clock Tom Valley felt that everything had been arranged most satisfactorily. A photographer friend had made copies of each letter, and one of them was already in the post to Dr. Drozd at the Soviet Embassy. The letters themselves had been safely deposited with his bank, and he had also telephoned Hyde, Herod & Scott who were perfectly willing to allow him a preview of the Vitgeft library some time next week. He was quite pleased with himself as he came back to the shop.

"Hullo, Mr. Valley. It's been very quiet today, I'm afraid." His assistant, a girl of sixteen, smiled sadly at him. "Don't think I've taken more than a quid since lunch."

"That's all right, Anne. It's always quiet on Mondays, and as I've told you, the postal trade is what we've got to worry about. Just keep your fingers crossed—I'm hoping to do a nice bit of business soon. If I do I'll buy you a new coat."

"Cor, thanks, Mr. Valley. I could certainly use one." Anne glanced with disgust at her own worn garment hanging by the desk.

"An old gentleman left these for you to look at just after you went out. I said they weren't any good, but he told me I didn't know my business, and he'll be back to see you about them in the morning."

"Did he? Well, let's have a look." Tom bent over the sorry collection of books she had piled on the table and glanced at the spines.

"No, you know your business all right." He frowned slightly and then pushed the books to one side. Forgotten novels with worn and damp-stained covers, battered Victorian calf with the leather looking like dry sponges, two odd volumes of *The World's Masterpieces of Literature*. Just junk, and he could imagine the kind of house that they came from. Poverty disguised by the brass companion set before the fire—the oiled aspidistra—the illuminated testimonial "Presented after forty years of devoted service" hanging in the parlour. He could also imagine the annoyance in their owner's face as he rejected the books. Annoyance and hurt dignity, as though this rejection was also a slur on his own taste and culture.

"No, we certainly don't want to be landed with any of these, do we? Anything else come along while I was out?"

"There wasn't anything important, Mr. Valley, though Miss Bond rang up about an hour ago." There was a slight bitterness in the girl's voice. Though she liked Florrie, she also felt extremely jealous of her.

"Did she leave any message?"

"Yes, I've got it down here." Anne picked up a piece of paper from the desk. "I couldn't really understand it, but it was something about some letters she'd given to you on Satur-

day. She said that on no account must you show them to anybody till she'd spoken to you. She's going to try and ring you
tonight, but it may be late as she's tied up at the office."

"I see. Thanks, Anne." Tom sat down wearily behind the
desk. He didn't see at all. They'd talked it over so carefully,
agreed on everything—why should Florrie change her mind
now? All the same, he had spoken to Drozd about the letters
and there was nothing he could do about it. He couldn't even
phone her either, as the department's number was as heavily
screened as that of Buckingham Palace. The chances were
that she'd be working till midnight over this Kapitza business
as well. He'd just have to sweat it out till she got in touch with
him.

"And now you push off, Anne," he said. "I've got a couple
of letters to write and there's no point in both of us hanging
about when it's as quiet as this. I'll be shutting up in a few minutes anyway."

He watched her gather up her belongings and go out, and
he cursed his luck. No, there would be no easy pickings, no
jackpot for him this time. Florrie's message could only mean
one thing. She had found that the letters were already mentioned in the department's files, and they would have to be
returned at once. Damn—damn—damn! He felt like a bettor
who has put his all on the hundred-to-one outsider and finds
he has lost his slip as it romps past the post.

And as Anne had said, it was quiet, even for a Monday. He
took five shillings from the paperbacks on the outside shelves,
sold an outdated *Times Atlas* to an old lady who looked as
though she could scarcely carry it away, and answered two
enquiries from American dealers. By the time he had finished
he felt he had really had enough for the day.

"Evenin', old boy." He looked up with a jerk and saw two
men smiling at him in the doorway. "Is it all right by you if
we take a look around?" They were in their early forties and
both dressed alike: dark trilby hats pulled low down, belted
raincoats with whipcord trousers showing under them, and

thick brogue shoes. The one who spoke was perhaps a quarter of an inch taller than his companion and his moustache a little thicker, but the walking stick in his hand was his only real distinguishing mark.

"Yes, please look around, gentlemen," Tom said. "Though I'm afraid I'm closing in a few minutes."

"Thanks, old boy, and just you turf us out whenever you feel like it."

Their outdated slang sounded terribly forced, and Tom felt that he recognized the type at once. Two ageing, military Peter Pans whose lives had fruited for a short time during the war and now withered. The popular P.M.C. of the Officers' Mess, the life and soul at the regimental hops, the good scout in the German Control Commission or the Palestine Police, with a list of useful contacts in his pocket-book and a fiver in his wallet for a pal.

But the war had finished a long time ago, the dreaded word *redundant* had been pronounced, and under the trench coats and the stiff bearing there was a hint of seediness and weariness that seemed to tell of door-to-door selling and bed-sitting rooms in districts that had gone down and the longed-for days of the annual regimental reunion and endless military reminiscences in saloon bars. A sad, unfunny Tweedledum and Tweedledee whose battles were over, but never out of mind.

Yes, Tom fancied that he knew the type and he also knew that he had little chance of selling them a book. They were merely killing time till the pubs opened at six. He added up the day's takings, pulled back the door, and wheeled in the first of the outside cases. "Well, gentlemen, I'm very sorry, but I'm closing now," he said.

"Yes, so I see, but that's quite all right, Mr. Valley." The man with the stick put the book he was holding back on its shelf and smiled at him, showing a line of badly stained teeth as he did so.

"You know my name?"

"Yes, of course. No mystery about that, is there? Saw it

outside as we came in. 'Thomas Valley, R.B.A.' I suppose that stands for Rare Book Dealers' Association. Let me give you a hand, though." He helped Tom bring in the last case and then reached out and released the Yale catch so that the lock slipped forward to secure the door.

"Yes, that's better, isn't it—much better? All nice and private, so that nobody can come barging in to disturb us. And now, I think you've got a couple of rather valuable letters to give me, old boy."

"Letters! But I don't understand." Tom could only stare foolishly at those grinning, stained teeth. They were like crumbling pebbles mingling with the brown of the moustache. "Just who are you and how do you know about them?"

"Can't you guess who we are, Mr. Valley? You're very dense if you can't, I think. F.O. Intelligence wallahs, of course, but don't ask us for credentials as we never carry 'em. On the other hand, there's no need to take my word for it. You have a girl-friend named Florrie Bond who works in our department and the name of her boss is General Charles Kirk. Last Saturday Miss Bond removed two letters from the house of a woman who had been murdered and gave them to you. We've been sent over to collect those letters. That satisfy you?

"But it's still a bit public in here, isn't it?" The man looked at the glass door. "Haven't you got an office or something at the back where we could talk?"

"Yes, yes, there's a flat through there." Tom turned and led them towards it. He felt nothing except utter dejection. He'd built his hopes on those letters and lost them. Now they were really in the soup and Florrie might well lose her job—if nothing worse happened. He cursed his stupidity in even imagining they could have got away with it.

"Ah, that's much better." The man with the stick smiled at the little office-cum-living-room. "Small perhaps, but very nice and cosy. All right by you if I sit down for a moment, old boy? Got rather a gammy leg." He lowered himself onto a chair. As he did so, his companion opened the doors leading into the kitchen and bedroom. "The name's Topper, by the way.

"And don't mind old Blackie, Mr. Valley. He's rather a nervous character, I'm afraid, very cloak-and-dagger, and wants to make sure that we're alone.

"Everything okay, Blackie? Good. Now, old boy, would you just hand over those letters please?"

"I haven't got them here. I put them in the bank till tomorrow." Tom stared at the man's stick which was tapping against the toe of his shoe. There was something almost hypnotic about the way it bounced up and down on the polished leather—something unpleasant about the smile on his very ordinary face. He began to think he might have underestimated his visitors. They were strangely sinister and he wondered if the SS or the Black and Tans might not have been more suitable occupations for them than the Palestine Police or the Control Commission. Peter Pan hadn't merely aged, he'd grown vicious, too.

"In the bank, eh?" The smile faded slightly. "Very wise of you, old boy, though a nuisance for us, as we'll have to come back in the morning. Not important though, and this is what really matters. Have you shown these letters to anybody, or even discussed them with anybody except Miss Bond?"

Tom was about to answer that he'd shown them to Julius Rosen, but the chill in the smile made him change his mind. Why involve Julius in this, he thought. He noticed that the other man had moved back from the kitchen door and was standing just behind him.

"Mr. Valley, just who else did you show the letters to? Come on, I can tell from your expression that there was someone else."

"I quoted them to a man at the Russian Embassy. I didn't think there was any harm in it, you see. I sent him two photostat copies as well." Tom waited for some flicker of annoyance in the man's face, but all he did was smile again and the stick tapped a little more quickly against his shoe.

"No, perhaps you didn't think there was any harm in it, Mr. Valley. Perhaps you really are as stupid as that. All the same, I think, it was rather naughty of you. Not cricket in fact. What you've done is going to cause us a good deal of trouble and we don't like trouble, do we, Blackie?"

The stick in Topper's hand tapped twice more and then stopped tapping. His mouth was still set in a wide grin, but nobody could say that his eyes were smiling. Unloved and unloving eyes searching for a scapegoat to explain his own inadequacy. He raised the stick, his hand tightened, and it swung out like a flail.

But it wasn't the pain that mattered. Not pain, or shock, or the nausea sweeping over Tom, as the stick cut into his throat and crushed against his Adam's apple, or that smiling face before him that looked even more horrible because the features that contained it were so very ordinary. Not the mist flooding over his eyes, or his lungs fighting for air, or his legs starting to buckle.

All those things were there, of course, but they weren't important. It was disbelief that mattered. The knowledge that it hadn't happened—that it was a nightmare that would soon pass—that it couldn't have happened—not in England—not from people who worked with Florrie— He lay gasping on his knees for a moment, and then hands were on his shoulders and dragging him along the floor.

"Yes, it'll have to be the second arrangement after all, Blackie." Topper lowered his stick and got up from the chair, leaning heavily on it.

"Sorry about all this, Mr. Valley, but you were very foolish and will have to take the consequences. Don't worry though, it won't be painful at all. Old Blackie is—or rather was—a medical man. Major in the Army Medical Corps actually, before a little experiment went wrong. Carry on, Blackie." He nodded, and Tom felt his sleeve being pulled back and the tiny familiar stab of a hypodermic needle.

"Good." Topper looked through the doorway of the tiny

kitchen. He held himself very stiff and upright, and even in his agony Tom could see that he wore a corset. "Yes, very good, in fact. A nice big gas cooker with a slot meter ready to hand. We'll make sure it has a shilling in it." He jangled the coins in his pocket.

"About how long will it be before Mr. Valley passes out?"

"Couple of minutes should do it." Blackie had a warm pleasant voice with a slight drawl in it. "I gave him a full hundred units of zinc insulin. A very useful drug for people in our profession is insulin. Leaves no trace in the body, and not a coroner in the world could tell that he'd been doped. Pity you hit him though, Topper. It'll make quite a bruise, I'm afraid." He squinted professionally at Tom's throat.

"Yes, I know, but the bastard annoyed me." Topper bent over the desk. "It doesn't matter though, because a nice suicide note should hold the wolves off long enough for our purpose." He slipped a sheet of paper into the typewriter. As he did so, his eyes fell on the photostats that lay beside it.

"But look at this. He's left the prints of the letters nice and handy for us. That's one thing in Mr. Valley's favour at any rate." He glanced briefly at them and then struck a match. They darkened, curled, and glowed orange.

"That takes care of that, and it will be some time before the originals in the bank come to light. Enough time for us to be well on our way. Let's keep our fingers crossed about the copies he sent to the Embassy."

"Now, how shall we word our farewell letter? 'My Darling Florrie'? Is that how you would address Miss Bond, old boy? Not telling, eh?" He shook his head in mock sorrow at Tom's set face. "Still it will have to do." His fingers started to run professionally across the keyboard.

"'My Darling Florie, the letters were fakes—just worthless fakes—and I don't want to go on any longer.' I think we'll break off like that, as though emotion had got the better of you, Mr. Valley. Yes, really quite apt, though I say so myself."

But Tom could hardly hear him. Nothing made sense any

more. Nothing fitted together, except pain and the nightmare of disbelief, and the knowledge that, whoever they were, these men were about to kill him.

No, by Heaven they weren't! Not if he played his cards right. Through the waves of pain there was suddenly hope as he remembered what Blackie had just said. Insulin—zinc insulin! A drug, but it was a cure, too. Crystalline burning up the sugar in the blood and wasting it. Results: contraction—faintness—hypoglycemic coma. The results for most human beings, that was, but he was one of the few with an excess of sugar in his body. If the fools had only noticed the punctures on his arms they might have suspected he was a diabetic and thought of a different drug from insulin.

A hundred units though—a full hundred! That was one hell of a dose. At least a third more than he'd ever taken in his life. All the same, he might just make it. If they didn't stay with him too long, he might.

Contraction—faintness—coma. The reality would probably come soon enough, but he would have to act now. He braced himself against Blackie's arms, twisted madly on the floor as though in the last stages of a fit, and then went completely limp.

"Nice timing, Blackie. Almost two minutes exactly. What a genius medical science lost when they got you for pushing all that heroin." Topper's arms were also around Tom now; Tom's feet were dragging across the worn linoleum of the kitchen and his face was sliding into a black cave that smelled of burnt fat. He heard a coin rattle in the meter, the creak of a rusty tap, and another smell mingled with that of the oven. For a moment he held his breath and then forced himself to breathe the gas. If they were to leave him before his pulse stopped, he would have to play his part convincingly.

A hundred units though! Dear God, a full hundred! Even a diabetic couldn't stand that much insulin. The craving for sugar was like another drug which killed all pain, and the sound of the gas a distant waterfall. Beyond it he heard Topper's voice.

"Goodbye then, Mr. Valley, and no hard feelings, I hope." He seemed to be speaking from the end of an very long passage.

"All part of the day's work, you know." A hand touched his shoulder for a moment and footsteps started to move away. Just as they reached the door he heard the final goodbye:

"So long, old boy, and as I said, no hard feelings. Maybe we'll meet up again one day and have a good laugh about all this—in hell perhaps."

The Admiralty launch, M.L. 27, was as big as a fair-size pleasure steamer, but from her low deck the Soviet cruiser looked enormous.

Sophie Robinson stood with Trubenoff, just behind the group of V.I.P.'s who were waiting to welcome Kapitza. She felt a mixture of pride and fear as she looked up at the *Donskoi*. Pride for the towering hull which looked as though it would crush the launch as they came together; pride for the guns lying stiff and menacing against the evening sky; pride for the rocket pads beside each funnel. Pride for a ship which her own people had built. *Dimitri Donskoi*, the namesake of a crazy out-of-date auxiliary which had fought off three Japanese cruisers after Tsushima and gone down with her flags flying.

But fear was there, too. Fear of the scarlet ensigns at the mast, the doll-like figures on the bridge, and the group of sailors standing ready to lower the gangway. Sophie's face was almost plump now with the rubber pads filling out her cheeks, her hair was dark instead of blonde, and she wore thick-rimmed glasses, but she felt like a naked child as the launch wheeled on the swell and came to rest against the cruiser's side.

"And remember what I said, Sophie Petrovna. Point out any face which you think you may have seen before, even if you're not certain that it was at Koshuba." Trubenoff leaned forward slightly and gripped the rail as the launch shuddered and then came to a standstill. "Any face at all."

"Yes, I'll do that." She watched the gangway sliding down like an arm towards the group in front of them. In the centre of the group she could recognize the Lord Mayor of London, a face she must have seen a score of times in the financial papers; beside him, the Admiral commanding the Nore station—a hammer-and-pincers face, with the hooked nose almost meeting the jutting chin; to his right the Russian Ambassador and two dandified men from some ministry. Their faces were set in fixed smiles of welcome, but their eyes looked tense and strained.

And Kapitza was coming now. Orders were being shouted against the wind and the cries of gulls and the whine of the engines. There was a sudden rattle of side-arms, the sailors stood back from the gangway, and a little bearded man began to walk cautiously down towards them. She'd never thought that he'd be so small, though, or that the woman behind him would look so old and pathetic. A peasant woman with round weatherbeaten cheeks smiling shyly, with the wind tugging at her grey hair and the cotton dress that looked far too big for her. The woman whose birthday it was—a wife who might easily become a widow before her journey was finished.

"Atten-shun." British rifles crashed in salute and boatswain's pipes screamed. She watched the Lord Mayor remove his hat and bow very low, the Admiral raise a craggy hand in welcome, and the Ambassador fuss round like the *compère* of a stage show. Kapitza stumbled slightly as the launch wheeled offshore; then he walked towards the entrance of the saloon.

But other people were coming down the gangway now. Secretaries, interpreters, the captain of the cruiser, two obvious army officers looking stiff and uncomfortable in their civilian clothes. And behind them were the people she had come to watch.

But they all looked so alike. Quiet dark suits, hats pulled down low over high-boned Slavonic faces which seemed quite blank and indifferent—apart from the staring eyes which flickered over the launch and wouldn't be missing anything. The eyes of guard dogs which had been trained for just one duty and one skill. If Alderman Sefton-Palmer, Lord Mayor of London, did anything so unlikely as pulling a revolver from his pocket, she knew that he would be dead before he could fire it.

And Danilenko had said that one of those faces didn't belong to a watchdog, but to a wolf who was not there to guard but to kill. A paid assassin, a fanatic, a brainwashed automaton even, who would shoot down his master just before the launch reached Westminister Steps.

"Well Sophie, there they are. Do you recognize one of them?" Trubenoff leaned forward again and the scent of Egyptian tobacco from his mouth mingled with the smell of the sea. "Is there anybody whom you even think you might have seen at Koshuba?"

"No, no, not yet. But let me concentrate." She stared at the escort filing past them. Set, watchful faces—a dead white face that looked as though it had been buried under the earth for years—a face with a little scar below the mouth—a face which might have had the merest hint of a smile in its searching eyes.

"No, I don't remember seeing any of them before." She forced her mind back to Koshuba. The sweltering heat in the summer, and how the snow had piled up outside the windows in winter. The way the dogs had howled beside the barbed wire and how the searchlights swung from the towers all night long. Fear and pain and loneliness, though you were never physically alone. The dark shadows behind the lamps and the voices which always said the same things: "What did you tell him? How many times did you meet him? How much did he pay you for the information? How often? How much? How many times? Anything else—anything else—anything else?"

Then at last the voices had stopped, and the knowledge that she was free had come to her like a great blinding vision. There was suddenly no more pain and no more loneliness. There was nothing at all except peace and the need to be part of something again.

"No, I don't remember seeing any of them before," she said,

but even as she spoke, she knew that she had to remember. Everything depended on her remembering, and she couldn't let them down now. With the sweat cold under her arms and a sound like spinning clockwork in her head she studied the faces of Kapitza's bodyguard again. A white, buried face—a face with a scar—-a face which almost seemed as though it were smiling—a face which had the hint of flat Mongolian features mingling with those of the Slav.

A face with a scar! Yes, yes, that was what she had to remember. A face with a scar! A little white scar like the shape of the letter Y beneath the thin mouth, with the tail of the Y running down in a deep groove across the chin. A face with a scar which she was looking at now and making herself remember.

"Yes," she said. "Yes, I do remember. There is one of them who was at Koshuba. The third man on the left who is standing by the doorway—he was there." She felt Trubenoff's fingers touch her arm as she spoke and the deck shuddered under her feet as the engines of the launch quickened. They began to move off towards London.

CHAPTER FIFTEEN

He wasn't sure if they'd gone. He wasn't sure about anything except that death was very close. All the same, he had to trust his luck.

Very slowly Tom Valley began to pull his head out of the stove. His lungs were bursting bladders of poison, the sea smell of the gas fanned his hair, and the metal clawed at his face, but at last he was out of it. He crouched on the floor, kneeling before the oven like a worshipper at a shrine and then reached up for the tap.

But he couldn't make it. He couldn't even lift his hand to the tap. Without sugar he couldn't do anything. Though he'd beaten the gas for the time being, there was still another poison in his body—drying it up, burning out energy and life.

He had to have sugar or die. He pulled himself round and started to crawl forward on his hands and knees.

The kitchen was ten feet square, but it seemed like an acre. Now and then the floor lurched and reared up like a living thing to throw him sideways. Sometimes his arms gave way and he lay gasping at the poisoned air before dragging himself on. Six inches—a foot—a yard—eighteen inches—two yards. At last his hand reached the leg of a table which seemed to be clamped to the floor, but finally tilted as he threw his remaining strength against it.

Now where was it? His hands ran wildly over the things that had fallen around him. Broken dishes, a frying pan, part of a cup, and at last the one thing that could save life. A little blue tin lying on its side against the wall. He couldn't tell that it was blue, of course—his eyes only seemed able to make out reds and greys now, but he knew it was what he wanted. He dragged off the lid, seeing grey sand spew onto the floor, and buried his face in it, forcing his dry throat to swallow.

The sugar took effect quickly. Almost at once his body seemed to swell out and he felt strength coming back. His lungs were still bursting and a red-hot needle was boring into his skull, but he suddenly felt stronger than he ever had in his life, a giant who was beyond death. He pulled himself to his feet and staggered to the back door, turning off the gas as he did so.

But why? Just why—and who were they? He leaned against the wall of the yard, drawing in great gulps of air, and all tiredness left him as sugar and oxygen did their work. He felt like a man who has had almost exactly the right amount of alcohol to drink, and one more sip will show him the true face of God. Whoever those would-be killers were, he'd beaten them. The disease he'd always despised himself for had beaten them. Without diabetes he'd have been dead meat by now, rotting in his own stove with the gas still fanning his hair.

All the same—why—why—why? And who the hell were the bastards? He swayed drunkenly against the wall, staring up at the sky and trying to concentrate. They hadn't been British Intelligence officers, that was certain. Were they Russian agents then? Perhaps, but his mind just didn't seem able to work properly. He'd have to do something, though. The police? Yes, that was it. He should tell the police what had happened. He lurched back into the flat, knocking over a pile of books as he did so, but paused as he reached the telephone.

The police! What good would they do? Just a bunch of flat-footed oafs, swigging tea all day and stuffing themselves full of steak and two veg in the station canteen. No, he didn't want the police. This boss of Florrie's was the man who should be told. What was the fellow's name? Yes, Kirk—Colonel Kirk. He'd know what should be done all right. Or was it *General* Kirk? Still, what did rank matter? The important thing was to get in touch with him at once. He lifted the phone, staring foolishly at the mouthpiece for a moment, and then put it down. No, that was no good, he hadn't got the blasted number. There was an address though, if only he could remember it. Yes, it was coming back to him—Saint Agnes House, Southwark, Ministry of Foreign Affairs—Department 14—2nd Floor, Saint Agnes House, Southwark. Um, quite a handful, but that was the place for him, and he'd be on his way. He just hoped he could remember where he'd parked the car.

He pulled open the shop door, slamming it hard behind him, and hearing glass shatter as he did so, and marched unsteadily down the street. To keep his feet in line he aimed them at the joins of the pavement, and a childhood nursery rhyme ran through his head in a pleasant jingle—"Look, look, look at me, Bears. See how I'm walking between the squares." Yes, this Colonel Kirk was the man for him, and he'd have a thing or two to tell him all right.

The car was parked as he remembered. After three fruitless jabs with the key he found the lock and climbed in. The motor started with a firm powerful hum, and he let out the clutch and moved off, crumpling a fender against a lamp post as he did so.

He had a long way to go, and the chances were that he

wouldn't make it. To control the crowds which were pouring in to witness Kapitza's arrival, London was a maze of detours and every available police car would be on patrol. That scarred fender and his jerky, erratic driving would proclaim him "drunk" as though it were written on his number-plate.

No, it was about ten to one that he would never reach Saint Agnes House, and a hundred to one that he would get past the janitors. All the same, if he did get to Kirk, he might make history, and become much more than a beaten, drugged victim of a murder gang who had stumbled on a clue he didn't understand and escaped death by a miracle.

In a way he might almost be said to be Death himself. Death, the Conqueror—Death, the Avenger—on his pale horse which was a battered, pale blue, five-year-old but still not completely paid-for Morris Oxford saloon, riding down to London's river to save the world.

"Brr, it's freezing in here." Kirk scowled at the cold upper bars of his fire through a haze of cigar smoke. "You're sure we can't turn it on full, my dear?"

"No, I'm afraid not, sir." Florrie shook her head. "Triggs was quite definite. He said that if we used too much current the fuses would go."

"Did he indeed? Incompetent little jack-in-office. I shall look forward to having a word with Mr. Triggs in the morning. Sorry about this, Colonel. It makes me feel a very poor host."

"Not at all, General." Danilenko mopped his forehead with a handkerchief. In his opinion the room was stifling as it was, and he mentally blessed Mr. Triggs, whoever he might be. "But isn't it about time that we switched on the television?"

"We will in a moment, but there's no hurry. I always keep that clock five minutes fast." Kirk crossed to a cupboard in the corner of the room. "First I think we should have a little toast"—he filled two glasses, placing one in front of the Russian, and raised his own—"that your Mrs. Robinson won't let us down."

"Very well, I'll drink to that, General Kirk. Though I don't think there's any need to worry. Mrs. Robinson has been very thoroughly briefed and, if there is a killer on that boat, she'll spot him. Here's to everything going according to plan!" Danilenko lifted his arm and threw back the whisky in a quick practised movement. The glass looked as small as a thimble in his huge hand.

"Cheers!" Kirk emptied his own glass and turned to Florrie. "You've checked that our radio link with the launch is working all right?"

"Yes, sir, just five minutes ago when they were on their way out to the cruiser. It's connected to that white telephone on your desk and all you have to do is to lift the receiver."

"Good, then let's see if they've started yet." Kirk leaned forward and switched on the set. Almost at once the screen took on a picture: the Thames estuary with the evening sunlight glinting on the water, Southend pier like a thin wire stretching out to sea, and in the far corner a toy ship which was the *Dimitri Donskoi*.

". . . well, so far the timing of Kapitza's arrival has been quite stupendous." Well-fed, soothing, and assured, the announcer's voice floated across the room.

"At exactly six o'clock he transferred to the launch, and already they are well under way. Yes, we can see them now. Quite a little flotilla, isn't it? The M.L. with the Russian party in front, and just behind her the Trinity House launches, *Vixen* and *Viking*. And behind them—? Yes, that will be the *Cornflower*, the barge of the City of London Corporation. And to the left of her—to port I should say, is *Snapdragon*. She's one of the famous veterans of the Dunkirk evacuation, of course, and is carrying the Lords Lieutenant of Kent and Essex and representatives of the Government and the Trade Unions." A line of interference flickered across the screen, and then cleared to show a wedge of boats charging up-river with plumes of spray at their bows.

"And now I'm going to hand you over to Angus Duncan in

the BBC helicopter." The picture changed, making the boats look like insects clawing against the tide, and a Scots voice was speaking. It sounded blurred and indistinct under the rattle of the rotors.

"Good afternoon, ladies and gentlemen. I'm afraid we can't give you a very close view, as for security reasons we're only allowed within half a mile of the procession. However, you should get an idea of the scene or, rather, panorama, below us. That's Westcliff-on-Sea coming up now, and the shore is completely lined with small craft. There must be a thousand of them I should say, and every one almost smothered with bunting. Anybody who has anything that will float seems to have turned out today. However Kapitza's talks with the Prime Minister progress, he can't complain of his welcome this evening.

"By the way, it may interest you to know that your picture is coming to you by way of one of the new Haley-Moncelli lightweight transmitters. It must be almost the first time that this apparatus has been used for an air-to-land transmission, I think.

"And yes, they seem to be making excellent time. That's Canvey Island below us in the corner of the picture. Absolutely dead on schedule according to my watch—"

"The damn fellows might be reporting a boat race." Kirk turned away from the set and dragged at his cigar. At this stage of the proceedings he was only mildly interested. The attempt on Kapitza's life would not take place on the lower reaches of the Thames, but when the launch turned in towards Westminister and he came up on deck.

He looked across at Danilenko and wondered if he had done the right thing. He knew that there would be an attack on Kapitza in the launch, but had the assassins made other plans as well? All his security arrangements were based on the launch, and they would be wide open if another killer was stationed in a more conventional position. Once again he pictured a window sliding open to reveal a rifle. Once more he imagined what would happen to him if Kapitza died in England. "Click," ran the sound of billiard balls in his head, and loud came the whispered conversations from the hotel bars: "Funny old boy—was something once, I heard, but made a mess of it—just a has-been." Click—click—click.

"They are in the Thames proper now." The announcer's voice cut into his thoughts. "You can see Tilbury and Graves-end coming up. Ferry-boats moored on the banks and absolutely black with people. Everybody seems to have turned out." Different voices, different pictures, different positions as the launch ran on towards London.

"Greenhithe over there on the right now, and quite a large steamer anchored offshore— What's that, Peter? Oh, I see.

"Yes, that's interesting. My colleague, Peter Hathaway, tells me she is the Russian timber carrier, *Kamchatka*, quite a regular visitor to the Thames. This must be a great day for her crew. Almost to Woolwich now. Yes, that's the Royal Arsenal you can see on the right of your screen—"

"What on earth!" The announcer's voice was drowned by Kirk's bellow of astonishment. "And just who are you?" He glowered at the man who staggered into the room. A young man who seemed to be in the last stages of intoxication, and looked as though he had recently been in a brawl and got very much the worst of it. His eyes were glassy, there were long streaks of grime down one side of his face, and below his chin was a great swollen bruise of black and purple.

"Tom! Tom darling!" Kirk saw Florrie rush across the room and throw her arms around the apparition. "Darling, what's happened to you? What's been done to you?

"It's all right, General. I know him. He's a friend of mine, Tom Valley."

"It is not all right, girl." Kirk's voice might have been quelling a full-scale mutiny. "Just stand away from him, will you. Do as I say. Excuse me, will you, Colonel." He turned down the volume of the set, glancing at Danilenko who sat woodenly in his chair, as though such interruptions were an everyday occurrence for him.

"And now, young man, I'm waiting for your explanation. Just what do you want, and what do you mean by forcing your way into my office?"

"I had to come—I have to talk to you." Tom swayed against the wall as he spoke. "It's important, you see. The janitor was listening to the radio downstairs, so I sneaked past him. By the way, you are Colonel Kirk, I suppose?"

"Yes, my name is Kirk, and the rank is not important." Kirk's voice was quite different now, for as he studied Tom Valley he could see that he wasn't drunk but drugged.

"Now, please sit down and tell me what it is that you want to say?"

"They tried to kill me, Colonel. They came for the letters, and then they tried to kill me." The words came pouring out as Tom lurched across to a chair. "They said they were from British Intelligence."

"No, that's not the way, Mr. Valley. I can't understand you unless you start from the beginning. Florrie, will you please give your friend a glass of brandy? Now, take your time, Mr. Valley, and tell me exactly what happened."

Kirk's face was quite without expression as he listened to Tom's story, but his maimed hand drummed on the arm of his chair, and from time to time he glanced at the television. The boats were well past Greenwich now, with the masts of the *Cutty Sark* behind them. All the same there was still time.

"Yes, I see," he said. "Two men who referred to themselves as Topper and Blackie came to your shop and demanded certain letters which Miss Bond had taken from the house of Tania Vitgeft. Letters which you think may have been written by Karl Marx to Friedrich Engels.

"And when you told them that the letters had already been quoted to the Soviet Embassy, they attempted to kill you. Quite a clever attempt, too, which would certainly have succeeded had you not been a diabetic.

"Yes, you were quite right to come directly to me, Mr. Valley. Two letters written by Karl Marx and owned by a woman to whom his very name should have been anathema! All very, very curious." Once again he looked at the silent screen. They were getting closer now. That must be Poplar on the north bank and the Isle of Dogs, a tangled forest of cranes, to the south.

"But who were these men, I wonder? Not mine, I promise you, and they don't sound like Soviet agents either. What do you think, Colonel?" He turned towards Danilenko, but the man didn't even seem to be listening. He had got up from his chair now and was staring out of the window with his head sunk between his shoulders as though in deep thought.

"So let's try and find out for you, Mr. Valley. Let's see if our Records Department know of any unpleasant characters named Topper and Blackie?" Kirk's hand reached out across the desk; it didn't go towards the intercom, however, but to the little white telephone which was the radio link to the launch. He was within an inch of reaching it when Danilenko turned from the window.

"No, General," he said. "I wouldn't do that, if I were you. I wouldn't even think of trying to contact Mr. Trubenoff—not just for the moment at any rate." He smiled as Kirk's arm drew back.

"Thank you, that's much better. And now it's time that I introduced myself. Oh yes, my name is Boris Danilenko, but I was not a colonel of artillery as I told you, but of the Red Army Intelligence Service." He walked towards the desk and there was a heavily silenced pistol in his hand.

"But surely you can guess the rest of it. You see, my object in going to East Berlin was to receive orders as well as information—very clear orders." He gave a little stiff bow and his smile widened.

"Yes, General Kirk, I have the honour to be Michael Kapitza's executioner."

CHAPTER SIXTEEN

Just eight bridges to go and it would be finished. Sophie Robinson watched the long shadows of Tower Bridge creeping across the water, and then glanced at Trubenoff. On the surface he looked completely relaxed and at ease, almost indifferent in fact, though now and then his eyes flickered over the man she had pointed out to him. A pale, stolid man who leaned beside the door of the companion-way with the Y-shape scar she had claimed to have seen at Koshuba dead white against the grey pallor of his skin. A man she had never seen before in her life.

Yes, the British had swallowed the bait, and everything was working—just as they had told her it would work. As the launch swung in towards Westminster, Trubenoff's eyes would be fixed on that man, and nobody would notice when the real killer moved. Though she herself would most probably be dying with Kapitza, she had to admire the British.

Only seven to go now. The noise of the engines seemed to increase beneath each bridge, and the launch shuddered slightly as it breasted the tide race. Seven more bridges and Kapitza would come blinking out on deck for his execution.

"Any face that you knew at Koshuba." Over and over again they had said that, but it was nonsense, of course, for there was only one face that she could remember. That huge rock-like face with the neck muscles straining against the uniform collar, the eyes boring into her from beside the lights, and the voice which was usually harsh, but could sometimes be kind and gentle.

It had been kind the last time she had heard it in Russia, and the big hand had touched her shoulder like a caress. "And that's that," he had said. "That's all you need to learn, little

Sophie, and the treatment is over. You are quite free to go and marry your Englishman and nobody will stop you." She had never felt more strength and comfort in her life than she did from the touch of those hard, gentle fingers.

"Yes, my dear, it's over. You have been sick, but are quite well now, and there is just one thing for you to remember. Some day—perhaps in a month, a year, twenty years even—I will come and ask you to do me a service. And you will do it, won't you, Sophie? Just why will you do what I tell you?"

"Because—because—" The grey battlements of the Tower were sliding past now, and she heard her own voice answering and mingling with the whine of the engines, the rattle of the helicopter in front of them, and the whoop of ships' sirens from the Pool behind. Fifteen years had slipped away and she was giving her answer. The same answer that she had repeated to him in the farm-house just three days ago. "Because there is nothing in the world to be frightened of except you."

Yes, she'd learned her lesson well at Koshuba Camp. "Nothing in the world—nothing in the universe—nothing in heaven or hell. There is nothing to be frightened of—except you, Comrade Danilenko."

There was another bridge approaching now, London Bridge looking bare and empty without traffic or bystanders, and it told her that very soon Kapitza would be coming up from the cabin. As the launch ran towards the centre arch she clutched the strap of her handbag a little tighter and considered its contents. A comb, a mirror, a lipstick, a powder compact, a bunch of keys, a purse containing three pounds eight and sixpence, a crumpled packet of cigarettes, a cigarette lighter. Rather a wonderful cigarette lighter to those who knew its secret. On its side lay a raised silver star which, when pressed in a certain manner, would slide back to show a shining little muzzle that spat cyanide.

So, that was it! That was the truth at last. A crackpot league of Russian exiles who one day had received an injection of fresh blood into their ranks. What no one knew was that the blood belonged to the Soviet Intelligence Services.

Kirk stared at Danilenko. Though the man was his bitterest enemy, there was deep respect in his eyes. Ten years, he thought. Yes, for ten years you fooled us all; the police, the department, the bona fide members of the L.W.R., the politicians. For ten years you played your strutting, clanking clown's act while I called you Colonel Bogus and laughed at you. And all the time you were building up your organization.

He bowed stiffly across his desk. "Please allow me to offer you my congratulations," he said.

"Thank you, General, but I'm not sure that congratulations are called for." Danilenko still smiled, but it was a tired smile now with no bounce in it. The heavy face almost seemed to have grown transparent to show something old and weary behind.

"No, don't congratulate me, General Kirk," he said, "because I failed, you see. I failed badly. I made something and now I have to let you destroy it. I built up a spy ring which could have been unbeatable—a group of dedicated experts hiding behind clown's masks, with here and there one or two poor automatic instruments like Sophie Robinson. For ten years that was my work and now you will destroy it, merely because we didn't find those letters."

"Ah yes, the letters. Would you like to tell me about them, Colonel?" Kirk's hand began to slide across the desk. Time was all against them, but if he could keep Danilenko talking he might be able to reach the little automatic in his drawer.

"I'll tell you about them, but don't try anything, please." As though the Russian had read his thoughts, the gun came up. "I'll tell you all you want to know, but if you make one false move I'll kill you." Danilenko looked at the television screen again. The launch was through the Pool of London and moving on towards Blackfriars. "Yes, we have almost ten minutes, I think.

"Tania Vitgeft was one of us, of course—one of the best of

us. It was she who originally thought of filling the L.W.R. with our agents. Yes, old Tania was a very bright girl, but she had a dangerous hobby; she collected Socialist ephemera. Quite a valuable collection it must have been. Letters from Marx and Engels, one from Lenin, a diary that had belonged to Rosa Luxemburg. Too bad that we had to destroy it when she died."

"But why did you destroy it?"

"You should be able to guess that, Miss Bond." Danilenko smiled at Florrie. "If General Kirk knew of the existence of that collection he would have become suspicious, I think. Though he might not have thought at once that Tania was a Soviet agent, he would have felt it strange that a person with her anti-communist views should keep such a collection. And once he did that, he would have started to look a little closer into our affairs.

"And we couldn't allow that, you see. As long as people thought of us as a bunch of heel-clicking clowns, drinking toasts to the late Tzar, carrying out elaborate cloak-and-dagger operations which came to nothing, offering worthless help to Russian deserters, we were safe. But let them once look at us without a smile, and they'd know the truth. Correct, General?"

"Yes, quite correct." As Kirk looked at him he felt a wave of self-disgust. You fool, he thought, you old blind fool. For years you laughed at them—you joked about them—you thought they were just an annoying rabble of harmless eccentrics. And all the time, right under your nose—

"But tell me, Colonel," he said. "It was you who killed Vitgeft, of course?"

"Well, shall we say that I arranged for her to die. I didn't like doing it, but there was no choice. Over a year ago certain people in Moscow decided that Kapitza was to be liquidated if he ever left the Soviet Union, and my organization was asked to take on the job. Naturally I discussed this with my senior colleagues and all of us agreed, except Tania. She said that her loyalties were with Kapitza, and she threatened to inform his security people about our plans.

"And so she died. There was nothing at all difficult about that, and we left a nice false trail for good measure. A woman dressed up like Tania and boarded the train to Edinburgh in her place. Just before the train reached its destination she changed back into her own clothes and walked off.

"Two mistakes were made, though. The men who killed her were supposed to remove the body, and destroy her collection, but they were disturbed by a meter reader and left the body in a trunk. Also, they failed to find two letters. Yes, the letters you told me about, Miss Bond, and which will certainly be my death warrant."

"Your death warrant!" Florrie spoke quite automatically. She wasn't looking at Danilenko, but at the switches of Kirk's fire. If she could reach them, there might still be a chance of saving Kapitza.

"Oh yes, my dear, those letters certainly will kill me." Danilenko's voice sounded as though he were stating an unpleasant but rather dull fact. "I knew that as soon as you spoke to me about them this afternoon. I sent my men round to Mr. Valley's shop to get hold of them and make sure that he wouldn't talk. As it happened, they failed on both counts. Not very efficient killers, I'm afraid, but it's difficult to get reasonable human beings for that type of work, as you probably know, General. Still, it doesn't matter now. Very soon the Russian Embassy will learn the truth, just as you have already done, General Kirk, and the organization will be wiped out.

"No, you were the person who mattered, Miss Bond, and that is why I am here now. I couldn't risk your disregarding my instructions and talking to General Kirk about the letters, so I've stayed to the end. Had things been different, I would have made an obvious excuse not to come to the office. As it is, I have to wait and see that Mrs. Robinson is allowed to finish her job." He shrugged his shoulders. Kirk could imagine how his escape had been planned: a quick drive out into the country and an aeroplane waiting at some private field.

"Yes, as it is, I have to wait here and make quite certain that the pig dies." Once again his eyes swung towards the screen. Kapitza was on deck now, raising his hand and smiling at the crowded banks of the river. Kirk thought he could recognize Sophie Robinson a few feet behind him. There were less than five minutes to go.

"But why? Why do you want to kill him? He's a Russian, isn't he, like you?" Tom Valley was still half under the drug and his brain felt like a nerveless mass of cotton wool. He only vaguely realized what was going on, but he knew that this man had to be stopped.

"Yes, he is a Russian, Mr. Valley, but not like me." Danilenko looked at him and he wasn't smiling any more.

"I am a real Russian—a Stalinist Russian—and all my life I have fought for the Revolution. At Tzaritsin I fought for it when I was just a boy; in the Crimea and at Stalingrad I fought for it, and in Spain in the twenties. I have given my whole life for that dream of World Revolution. Do you think I would let Michael Kapitza destroy it now?

"And there are more like me—lots more—though many of us died or were broken and Kapitza's creatures control most of the M.V.D. and armed forces by now. Men like Gregor Durkin who will be arrested the moment the news breaks, but will probably die laughing when he knows we won. Yes, once it was decided to liquidate Kapitza outside Russia, I offered myself and my organization for the job and, though we are finished, we have done what we set out to do—to protect the dream of our Revolution which that weak man would like to abandon." His huge body seemed to swell with pride and he raised his hand in an almost theatrical gesture.

"Now, would you please turn up the volume again, Miss Bond, as I would like to hear the end of the story."

"As you wish." Florrie reached for the knob and then eased forward her chair till her foot was almost against the fire. If only the circuit is heavily loaded, she thought. If only Triggs' warning device works—if only—

"And here at Westminister Steps the official party, headed

by the Duke of Essex, is waiting to welcome Michael Kapitza."
There was more than a hint of excitement in the announcer's
voice.

"Yes, there is the Duke now, a resplendent figure in his uniform of Colonel-in-Chief of the Greys. The Prime Minister
just beside him, and behind him the Leader of the Opposition.
All waiting to welcome this man from whom we are hoping
so much.

"And we should see him very soon, I think. Yes, two minutes
to the hour and at any moment the launch should be coming
under Hungerford Bridge and turning in towards us. Yes, yes,
there they are now. She's moving very fast indeed—you can
see the spray at the bows, and the Red Flag and Union Jack
flying together—and—"

But Florrie didn't wait any longer. This was the last chance
and she had to take it. She kicked the switch of the fire, hoping
that the tiny click it made would be hidden by the television.
The bars darkened, glowed orange, darkened again, and she
heard the sound she had prayed for. A scream like that of a
stuck pig dying in agony—a soul in the last stages of some
unbearable torture. She saw Danilenko swing towards it and,
as he did so, she picked up Kirk's inkstand and flung it full in
his face.

And then Tom had him. He had him tight round the wrist,
hanging from it like a terrier on a bull's ear, with the huge face
that dripped ink glowering at him, and its mouth cursing him,
and arms whirling him around to crush his body against the
wall.

But he had to hang on. Danilenko was a mountain, beating
out his life, but he had to hang on to that gun. He swung round
with his feet off the floor, his back flailing against a table, and
he felt his fingers start to open. Then there was a noise like a
champagne cork popping, Danilenko's wrist went slack, and
stuff—wet stuff—spurted over his face.

"Don't worry, girl, he'll be all right." As Florrie rushed over
to Tom, Kirk laid down his gun and picked up the white tele-

phone. The fuses had blown and there was no sound or picture on the television now.

"Department Fourteen," he said. "Could I speak to Mr. Trubenoff, please? Oh, it is you, Igor. Yes, Kirk here. What's that you say? Yes, I see." His face was quite blank as he listened.

"Yes, I see, and there's no need to worry. As I told you, I'll take full responsibility. Very well, I'll ring you back in a few minutes."

He replaced the phone very slowly, and then bent down over Danilenko. The man was still alive, but he wouldn't be for long. Kirk's bullet had drilled a hole through the centre of his chest.

"Well, Colonel," he said, "it's over now, all over."

"Over! You say it's over?" The man's lips were grey now. "And I failed, didn't I? You got her before—" Even as he spoke Danilenko's eyes were beginning to glaze.

"No, I'm very sorry, but you didn't fail, Boris. You succeeded all too well." Kirk bent still lower over the huge dying head. "Can you hear what I'm telling you?

"Yes, that's right, you succeeded. You beat us all along the line. Exactly one minute before I called the launch, your Mrs. Robinson pulled out some kind of disguised gun and shot Kapitza in the back. They both died instantaneously."

"I'm sorry, General, I'm terribly sorry." Florrie could hardly look at Kirk as he got up and walked back to his desk. "I didn't know what the letters meant—what I was doing—neither of us did." She helped Tom to a chair.

"Yes, I'm sure you're sorry, my dear, but it doesn't matter at all." Kirk stared down at the huge body stretched out on the floor. Its dead eyes were open and they might have been smiling.

"If there is any blame it's my own. If I'd told you a little more this wouldn't have happened. Still, it's not important now, and you can keep the blasted letters, Mr. Valley. Sell them to the Soviet Government. I hope they pay you very well.

"And now will you please go and get somebody to clear up the mess in here."

"Yes, of course, sir, but—" Florrie had to tell him how she felt—that she knew what she'd done. If she had only realized what those letters meant, Kapitza would still be alive. His death meant two things: the world back in fear again, and Kirk broken. This would be the end for him all right. A scapegoat living alone with his shame. Living a long time probably. Three score years and ten didn't seem a great age any more these days.

"But what?" Kirk's colour was altering. A moment ago his face had been a dull unhealthy grey, but now a little flush was creeping back into his cheeks.

"My dear Florrie, you don't mean—you don't really think that—" He broke off and shook his head. The flush had become a dark angry glow.

"No, my girl, I can forgive you a good deal—removing those letters when I merely gave you permission to look at the books, cheating the public trustee—but I'm not going to forgive impertinence. You mean that you really thought Mr. Trubenoff and I were fools, did you? But pass me those matches, please. Thank you." He lit a cigar and scowled at her through the smoke.

"No, I'm not a fool, Miss Bond, and as far as I'm concerned the only thing that went wrong was when your Mr. Valley came barging in here and very nearly got all of us killed." He looked with loathing at Tom.

"But this is roughly what happened. Danilenko fooled us for a long time, but at the end he tried to play it too smart. Without my help he couldn't get his killer onto the launch so he took a chance and let me meet Mrs. Robinson. That gave the show away at once. Good God, woman, do you think I can't recognize a poor brain-washed automaton when I see one?

"No, I spotted what Mrs. Robinson was, and Mr. Trubenoff and I took precautions. We didn't know exactly what Danilenko was up to, of course, so we kept our suspicions very quiet and hoped he'd play into our hands. As it happened he did so. By tomorrow morning every agent of the L.W.R. will be under lock and key and the Soviet police who are loyal to Kapitza will know exactly what his friends in Moscow hoped to do to him."

"Then you mean . . . ?" Florrie could only stammer as she looked at him.

"I mean that we took precautions as I told you. While Mrs. Robinson was putting on her disguise, her handbag was searched and the weapon was found and rendered harmless. Igor Trubenoff told me the rest of the story just now. She fired it at Kapitza and went completely berserk when nothing happened. Tried to go for him with her nails. Doubtless my good friend, the Minister, will have something to say to me on that score, but I don't suppose I'll lose too much sleep over it."

"Then you mean that Kapitza is alive!" Florrie clutched Tom's hand in relief.

"Alive! Of course the fellow is alive, unless he fell into the river stepping ashore and got drowned. But that's hardly my responsibility.

"Look for yourself, though." Somebody must have replaced the fuses, for there was a picture on the television again. In it they could see the launch drawn up before the landing stage and a procession of cars driving away.

"Then why, General—why did you tell Danilenko that . . . ?" Florrie kicked off the fire before Mr. Triggs' warning device could resume action.

"Why did I tell him that he had succeeded? My dear girl, don't you even understand that?" Kirk looked down at the smiling face on the carpet.

"Danilenko was a nasty piece of work, but he was dying, wasn't he? He'd lost everything. He knew that by tomorrow the organization he'd taken ten years to build would be destroyed completely. What harm did it do me to let him die in peace?" He stood up and laid his torn hand on her shoulder.

"Florrie, my dear, Miss Colman comes back tomorrow, so your efficiency and your business ethics will be no concern of mine. But please, please, try to learn to have a little compassion."

www.ingramcontent.com/pod-product-compliance
Lightning Source LLC
Chambersburg PA
CBHW020023030726
47499CB00007B/2243